JANE AUSTEN'S FASHION BIBLE

More of Jane Austen's work available from
Macmillan Collector's Library

Sense and Sensibility

Pride and Prejudice

Mansfield Park

Emma

Northanger Abbey

Persuasion

Sanditon, Lady Susan &
The History of England

JANE AUSTEN'S FASHION BIBLE

Edited and introduced by
ROS BALLASTER

MACMILLAN COLLECTOR'S LIBRARY

This collection first published 2025 by Macmillan Collector's Library
an imprint of Pan Macmillan
The Smithson, 6 Briset Street, London EC1M 5NR
EU representative: Macmillan Publishers Ireland Ltd, 1st Floor,
The Liffey Trust Centre, 117–126 Sheriff Street Upper,
Dublin 1 D01 YC43
Associated companies throughout the world

Introduction and section introductions copyright © Ros Ballaster 2025
Selection and arrangement copyright © Macmillan Publishers International Ltd. 2025

ISBN 978-1-0350-4912-7

The permissions acknowledgements on p. 189 constitute an extension of this copyright page.

All rights reserved. No part of this publication may be reproduced, stored in a retrieval system, or transmitted, in any form, or by any means (including, without limitation, electronic, mechanical, photocopying, recording or otherwise) without the prior written permission of the publisher.

1 3 5 7 9 8 6 4 2

A CIP catalogue record for this book is available from the British Library.

Casing design and endpaper pattern by Tiana-Jane Dunlop
Typeset in Bodoni by Jouve (UK), Milton Keynes
Printed and bound in China by Imago

This book is sold subject to the condition that it shall not, by way of trade or otherwise, be lent, hired out, or otherwise circulated without the publisher's prior consent in any form of binding or cover other than that in which it is published and without a similar condition including this condition being imposed on the subsequent purchaser. The publisher does not authorize the use or reproduction of any part of this book in any manner for the purpose of training artificial intelligence technologies or systems. The publisher expressly reserves this book from the Text and Data Mining exception in accordance with Article 4(3) of the European Union Digital Single Market Directive 2019/790.

Visit www.panmacmillan.com to read more about all our books and to buy them.

CONTENTS

Introduction vii

JANE AUSTEN'S FASHION BIBLE

Diamond Envy 1
Fashionable Travel 9
The Merry Widow 17
Talking Muslin 25
Boys and Bonnets 35
A Gracious Dance 43
Children First 51
Kensington Gardens 59
Belles and Balls 71
Petticoats, Pride and Prejudice 79
Walking to Meryton 87
Crape Expectations 95
Health and Horseback 101
Playing the Part 109
Pugs and Pelisses 117
Taking Likenesses 125
Christmas Carriages 133
Allies and Enemies 143

Falling at Lyme 151
Concerted Efforts 161
Sea Airs and Sanditon 175

Fashion Glossary 183
Sources & Permissions Acknowledgements 189
Acknowledgements 191

INTRODUCTION

Ros Ballaster

The first issue of *La Belle Assemblée, or Bell's Court and Fashionable Magazine*, published in February 1806, promises to lead its reader through the world of fashion:

> We shall furnish him with a chart that will govern his voyage in all the varieties of the course. We shall begin from the very point of embarkation. He will see a young country girl, with decent manners, good morals, and a careful education, enter upon a fashionable course. He will see her carried through the different scenes of the *Beau Monde*, and guided by a gay, seducing, artful woman of fashion. He will perceive, that the patroness understands her work, and is competent to the undertaking. She will point out examples instead of giving precepts; and presenting scenes and characters, leave her young pupil to draw her own inferences. In one word, and what includes the whole art of instruction, she does not teach her pupil, but leaves her more wisely to instruct herself.

This introduction to the journal and its contents was titled 'The Beau Monde or History of the New World. Chapter the First', as though it were a work of fiction, of a type very familiar to readers of the period: the courtship-to-marriage plot of the young girl coming to adulthood.

Jane Austen had turned thirty only two months earlier. 1805 had been a tough year with the death of her beloved father, George Austen, in January and the struggles of the now all-female household of two unmarried daughters and their mother, joined by their friend Martha Lloyd, to come to terms with their grief and escape the fashionable watering place of Bath, especially hated by Jane. They moved out in July 1806 and toured the Midlands and the south of England before taking lodgings in Southampton in the autumn of 1806.

Eventually, Edward, Jane Austen's most affluent brother, offered them a home on one of his estates: the bailiff's cottage in the village of Chawton in Hampshire. They moved in on 7 July 1809, an experience on which Austen may have drawn for her description of the Dashwood women moving into Barton Cottage in *Sense and Sensibility* (1811).

Jane had been writing fiction since she was a child. There were lively short pieces of comic satire to entertain family, and a satirical little novel in letters about a 'gay, seducing, artful woman of fashion', Lady Susan. Austen had even sold by proxy and through the offices of another brother, Henry, a novel to the publisher Benjamin Crosby in spring 1803, but Crosby failed to bring it into print. First versions of what were to become *Sense and Sensibility* ('Elinor and Marianne') and *Pride and Prejudice* ('First Impressions') were begun in 1795 and 1796, respectively.

But it was once she was settled into her forever home, and with her twenties behind her, that Jane's career as a novelist writing for publication took off. The following years saw extraordinary productivity with four mature and brilliant novels put into print to some critical success if not explosive popularity, before her untimely death at the age of forty-one of an undetermined illness (medical specialists suggest symptoms conversant with lupus) on 18 July 1817. Two more novels were published posthumously and there are a few manuscripts of works not published or not brought to completion.

It may be that once settled in their new home, and despite being short of money, the women in the Austen household found some comfort in looking at the fashion plates and discussing the fashions in the monthly magazine *La Belle Assemblée*, several of which are reproduced in this book. Women of genteel classes living close to poverty – like Jane and her family – were necessarily preoccupied with clothing since everything had to be made or mended. In the only surviving accounts we have of Jane's, kept in a diary for 1807, her largest area of expense, 27.4 per cent, was on 'Cloathing [sic] and Pocket' with laundry a close second at 18.3 per cent (Hilary Davidson, *Jane Austen's Wardrobe*, p. 11). The letters that survive refer to clothing often: not only in terms of domestic economy but also reflecting on what is fashionable or can be made to be so. She and her sister Cassandra exchange vigorous correspondence about buying suitable lengths of material for having dresses made up, what to wear at balls and parties, trimming bonnets: always with an eye to thrift alongside elegance. Characters on tight budgets are often shown finding means to aspire to fashion in Austen's fictional world: the Steele sisters in *Sense and Sensibility*, when staying with the privileged and wealthy Lady Middleton, are described 'taking patterns of some elegant new dress, in which her appearance the day before had thrown them into unceasing delight.' Pattern gowns were fitted gowns taken as a template and copied in fabric, either cotton or linen lining cloth, to make a pattern for a new dress. This is, though, more satire about sycophancy than it is praise of domestic economy.

Austen's fiction is in fact short on detail about what her

heroines wear. It is a sign of silliness or vulgarity when a woman starts to rattle on about such matters, subject to mockery by the men – such as Henry Tilney or Fitzwilliam Darcy – who are deemed suitable matches for Austen's heroines. And those heroines are themselves often country girls finding their way in the new worlds of the beau monde. We as Austen's readers have as our guide through these stories a woman who, like the putative 'patroness' of *La Belle Assemblée*, knows her art and guides us through the stories without being tendentious, authoritarian or tedious. Designing and making texts and textiles is an intricate craft and most successful when it dresses its subject to advantage rather than shows off its own labour. This both Jane Austen and the modiste editors of *La Belle Assemblée* knew well. Both give us a sense that they are inviting us into real lives while of course they are also indulging outrageous fantasies of romance: from Elizabeth Bennet's securing property-rich Mr Darcy with his £10,000 per year income to the impossibly slender figure afforded to post-partum ladies by the Circassian corset introduced to readers by *La Belle Assemblée* in Summer 1814 (July 1814; fashions for August 1814).

    This book pays due homage to the aesthetic achievement of both the fashion journal, the makers whose skills it showcased and the fiction Austen spun about women's lives. Austen was not a historical novelist: her fictions were set in the present, or close to it. Fashion plates have been carefully selected to illustrate the fashions of the time and to visualize some of Austen's most striking scenes and characters. Along the way, I explore and explain the choices available in terms of textile and style, whether according to season (Austen's novels are carefully plotted by chronology), place (seaside resorts, London, small towns, balls, drawing-rooms) or activity (walking, travelling, riding, painting, dancing). I begin with extracts from her earliest teenage writings, trace the fashion disasters and triumphs in her major works, and finish by looking out to the vanishing prospects of health and healing at a fashionable seaside resort in her last, unfinished, and potentially finest work of fiction, *Sanditon*.

To be fashionable was not just to be well-dressed; it was also to be well-read and well-informed. The magazine included regular features that covered contemporary biography, extracts from fiction, poetry, music, reviews and news concerning politics and theatre. It usually contained, though, at least two fashion plates and 'explanation' about these fashions and fashions in general. Readers could purchase two parts separately, the first containing these print materials and usually two plates about matters other than fashion and the second consisting of the fashion plates illustrating what to wear in the next month and sewing patterns, with up to four pages of description of the plates, followed by 'General Observations on Fashion and Dress'. *La Belle Assemblée* gave in to competition when it announced the introduction of hand-coloured fashion plates in a double issue published on 1 January 1807. The proprietor, John Bell (1745–1831), addressed his subscribers, telling them that he had hoped to give them 'an opportunity of practising and improving their taste in the Fine Arts' by themselves, colouring the prints while maintaining the clarity of the lines of the engraving. However, he now offered them the opportunity to decide whether to purchase them coloured at an extra shilling for each number. The next issue on 1 February would be 'enriched in a very extraordinary style, with a *Transparent and lucid Print in Colours*, as a Specimen of the Fashionable, and very interesting, mode of colouring Prints to represent the effects of Stained Glass.'

The magazine was designed, then, to piece together an

elegant woman and to bring her to life in vivid colour. 'Elegance' is a word Austen places very carefully in her fiction. Emma describes Mrs Weston, the woman who was her much-loved governess, now married to a local gentleman, as having manners with 'propriety, simplicity, and elegance'. In the same chapter, pushy, affluent, vulgar Mrs Elton is described as 'elegantly dressed'. It is a word that features frequently in *La Belle Assemblée*; not only in its 'explanation' of the 'prints of fashion' for the next month inserted towards the end of each number. It was equally frequent in the 'General Observations on Fashion and Dress', the column that noted rising and sinking hemlines and waists, puffing and narrowing or absence of sleeves, newly designed accessories, and seasonal trends. In discussion of fashions for November 1811, we hear of the 'comet hat and mantle' – both decorated to suggest the streaming tail and starry point of the Great Comet of 1811, visible to the naked eye in the sky for nine months from the end of March, with its closest Earth approach in October. 'Such fashions as these are merely local, but the elegance and taste of both the hat and mantle are unrivalled, and we think it a pity they had not a title which might not have rendered them more durable favourites of the approaching winter.'

John Bell was the magazine's proprietor throughout the period when Austen became a published novelist (from 1806 until he stepped down in 1821). Like Austen's male publishers Thomas Egerton and John Murray, he seems to have an eye for gifts in women, not only in inviting talented female writers such as Elizabeth Inchbald and Caroline Norton to edit, but also in offering innovative 'modistes' to promote their designs in the pages. The most remarkable woman associated with the magazine, though, was his daughter-in-law, Mary Ann Bell, a fashion designer and editor with a real flair for diversifying markets and promoting her products, whose editorial star rose in the period that Austen's novels started to appear in print. She was not elevated to the role of fashion editor until 1811, when a breach between father and son was healed: John junior had launched rival magazine *Le Beau Monde* just eight months after the first issue of *La Belle Assemblée* was published on 1 March 1806. In April 1809, John Bell junior sold off his share and was declared bankrupt in June 1810. Mary Ann swiftly got back in her father-in-law's good books. Her distinctive style – energetic, vivid, cheerfully flattering – colours the pages of the magazine from October 1811 until John Bell senior retired in 1821. She set up her own salon in early 1814 at 22 Upper King Street in London and moved it to Charlotte Street a few months later. *La Belle Assemblée* placed Mary Ann's products too: the 'Chapeau Bras', a face-framing hat, first featured in the March 1814 issue; the Circassian corset was promoted in August 1814, unboned for ladies after pregnancy and to facilitate discreet changing at bathing resorts; and the 'Bathing Preserver' for September 1814, a long (morning) dress with an attached cap of light material(s) to be carried in a silk bag at the seaside. Like Jane Austen, Mary Ann Bell had a passion to improve and advance her profession without being prosy or preachy.

 La Belle Assemblée thrived for much longer than Jane Austen herself, continuing after Bell's retirement with some variations of title until it ceased publication in 1848. Austen's fiction has had a longer afterlife and posterity despite her short comet of a life; what we continue to value in her fiction is its lightly worn wisdom about human frailty and potential. Resourceful feminine design lay at the heart of the work of both.

JANE AUSTEN'S
FASHION BIBLE

DIAMOND ENVY

JANE AUSTEN COMPOSED *LESLEY CASTLE*, A SPOOF 'NOVEL IN LETTERS', WHEN SHE WAS SIXTEEN. HERE, MARGARET LESLEY, RAISED IN A REMOTE SCOTTISH CASTLE, WRITES TO HER FRIEND CHARLOTTE LUTTERELL ABOUT A VISIT TO LONDON.

Margaret and her sister Matilda are husband-hungry young women unable to come to terms with their new stepmother, Lady Lesley. Lady Lesley dresses herself up for small 'routs' and parties, decking herself in their mother's jewels in a manner which recalls the requirements to glitter and sparkle at the Georgian court.

'Court dress' was required to be worn when attending Queen Charlotte's court. While side panniers were no longer mandated after 1760 when George III took the throne, his wife Queen Charlotte (the couple married on 8 September 1761) insisted on round hoops so that the high waist was retained, producing a strange and awkward shape. Women were also required to wear white ostrich feathers with long lappets. *La Belle Assemblée* describes the court dress for February 1808 as adorned with diamonds. Diamonds were especially rare stones: mined in India and Brazil and stockpiled by jewel traders to increase their attraction. Majestic Margaret imagines herself to be a diamond of the first water whose lustre is frustratingly eclipsed by her showy little stepmother.

FASHIONS

FOR

FEBRUARY, 1808

EXPLANATION OF THE PRINTS OF FASHION

ENGLISH COSTUME
NO. I – THE MOST SPLENDID AND ELEGANT COURT-DRESS

A white satin petticoat, covered with gold spangle scaling, ornamented round the bottom and draperies, with a deep border of white velvet, embroidered in an elegant pattern of gold; and finished with a rich fringe of the same. Body and train of purple velvet, trimmed with a similar fringe; pocket-holes ornamented with a rich gold cord and tassels. Crescent stomacher of gold mosaic, finished with a splendid diamond brooch; front of the sleeves ornamented with the same.

Diamond necklace, earrings and bracelets. Hair *à-la-Madonna*, ornamented with a gold net; confined at the back of the head with a diamond comb and star, from whence descend court lappets of Brussels lace. Two curled ostrich feathers placed towards the left side. Plain tucker of lace corresponding with the lappets, brought to a point at the centre of the bosom. Shoes of ruby velvet, embroidered and trimmed with gold. Gloves of superfine French kid, worn above the elbow. Fan of carved ivory, with ruby stud; mount of ruby crape, richly embroidered with gold and spangles.

A Lady of Quality in the Birth day Court Dress

Extract from

LESLEY CASTLE

Letter 10
MISS MARGARET LESLEY TO MISS CHARLOTTE LUTTERELL

❖   ❖   ❖

Portman Square, April 13th

My dear Charlotte – We left Lesley Castle on the 28th of last month, and arrived safely in London after a journey of seven days; I had the pleasure of finding your letter here waiting my arrival, for which you have my grateful thanks. Ah! my dear friend, I every day more regret the serene and tranquil pleasures of the castle we have left in exchange for the uncertain and unequal amusements of this vaunted city. Not that I will pretend to assert that these uncertain and unequal amusements are in the least degree unpleasing to me; on the contrary, I enjoy them extremely and should enjoy them even more were I not certain that every appearance I make in public but rivets the chains of those unhappy beings whose passion it is impossible not to pity, though it is out of my power to return. In short, my dear Charlotte, it is my sensibility for the sufferings of so many amiable young men, my dislike of the extreme admiration I meet with, and my aversion to being so celebrated both in public, in private, in papers and in print shops, that are the reasons why I cannot more fully enjoy the amusements so various and pleasing of London. How often have I wished that I possessed as little personal beauty as you do: that my figure was as inelegant; my face as unlovely; and my appearance as unpleasing as yours! But ah! what little chance is there of so desirable an event; I have had the smallpox, and must therefore submit to my unhappy fate.

    I am now going to entrust you, my dear Charlotte, with a secret which has long disturbed the tranquillity of my days, and which is of a kind to require the most inviolable secrecy from you. Last Monday se'night Matilda and I accompanied Lady Lesley to a rout at the Honourable Mrs Kickabout's; we were escorted by Mr Fitzgerald, who is a very amiable young man in the main, though perhaps a little singular in his taste – he is in love with Matilda. We had scarcely paid our compliments to the lady of the house and curtseyed to half a score different people when my attention was attracted by the appearance of a young man, the most lovely of his sex, who at that moment entered the room with another gentleman and lady. From the first moment I beheld him, I was certain that on him depended the future happiness of my life. Imagine my surprise when he was introduced to me by the name of Cleveland – I instantly recognised him as the brother of Mrs Marlowe, and the acquaintance of my Charlotte at Bristol. Mr and Mrs M. were the gentleman and lady who accompanied him. (You do not think Mrs Marlowe handsome?) The elegant address of Mr Cleveland, his polished manners and delightful bow, at once confirmed my attachment. He did not speak; but I can imagine everything he would have said had he opened his mouth. I can picture to myself the cultivated understanding, the noble sentiments and elegant language which would have shone so conspicuous in the conversation of Mr Cleveland. The approach of Sir James Gower (one of my too numerous admirers) prevented the discovery of any such powers by putting an end to a conversation we had never commenced and by attracting my attention to himself. But oh! How inferior are the accomplishments of Sir James to those of his so greatly envied rival! Sir James is one of the most frequent of our visitors, and is almost always of our parties. We have since often met Mr and Mrs Marlowe but no Cleveland – he is always engaged somewhere else. Mrs Marlowe fatigues me to death every time I see her by her tiresome conversations about you and Eloisa. She is so stupid! I live in the hope of seeing her irresistible brother tonight, as we are going to Lady Flambeau's, who is, I know, intimate with the Marlowes. Our party will be Lady Lesley, Matilda, Fitzgerald, Sir James Gower and myself. We see little of Sir George, who is almost always at the gaming-table. Ah! my poor fortune, where art thou by this time? We see more of Lady L., who always makes her appearance (highly rouged) at dinner-time. Alas! what delightful jewels will she be decked in this evening at Lady Flambeau's! Yet I wonder how she can herself delight in wearing them; surely she must be sensible of the ridiculous impropriety of loading her little diminutive figure with such superfluous ornaments; is it possible that she cannot know how greatly superior an elegant simplicity is to the most studied apparel? Would she but present them to Matilda and me, how greatly should we be obliged to her. How becoming would diamonds be on our fine majestic figures! And how surprising it is that such an idea should never have occurred to *her*. I am sure if I have reflected in this manner once, I have fifty times. Whenever I see Lady Lesley dressed in them, such reflections immediately come across me. My own mother's jewels, too! But I will say no more on so melancholy a subject. Let me entertain you with something more pleasing – Matilda had a letter this morning from Lesley, by which we have the pleasure of finding that he is at Naples, has turned Roman Catholic, obtained one of the Pope's Bulls for annulling his first marriage and has since actually married a Neapolitan lady of great rank and fortune. He tells us, moreover, that much the same sort of affair has befallen his first wife, the worthless Louisa, who is likewise at Naples, has turned Roman-Catholic and is soon to be married to a Neapolitan nobleman of great and distinguished merit. He says that they are at present very good friends, have quite forgiven all past errors and intend in future to be very good neighbours. He invites Matilda and me to pay him a visit to Italy and to bring him his little Louisa, whom both her mother, stepmother and he himself are equally desirous of beholding. As to our accepting his invitation, it is at present very uncertain; Lady Lesley advises us to go without loss of time; Fitzgerald offers to escort us there, but Matilda has some doubts of the propriety of such a scheme – she owns it would be very agreeable. I am certain she likes the fellow. My father desires us not to be in a hurry, as perhaps if we wait a few months both he and Lady Lesley will do themselves the pleasure of attending us. Lady Lesley says no, that nothing will ever tempt her to forgo the amusements of Brighthelmstone for a journey to Italy merely to see our brother. 'No,' says the disagreeable woman; 'I have once in my life been fool enough to travel, I don't know how many hundred miles, to see two of the family, and I found it did not answer; so deuce take me if ever I am so foolish again.' So says her ladyship, but Sir George still perseveres in saying that perhaps in a month or two they may accompany us.

 Adieu, my dear Charlotte,
  Your faithful
   MARGARET LESLEY

FASHIONABLE TRAVEL

Kitty, or The Bower was begun in 1792 when Jane Austen was sixteen and revised between 1815 and 1817 by her teenage nephew James Edward, who used the full name of Catharine for the heroine.

Here, lonely novel-reading Catharine is getting to know her distant cousin Camilla Stanley, whose family has just swept up to Catharine's home in their coach-and-four for an extended visit. Camilla's obsession with fashion and her ignorance of geography, literature, history and politics become evident as she airs her plans for an upcoming trip to the North of England in the autumn. Camilla is not interested in looking at nature but rather in being looked at herself. She concentrates her wardrobe plans on a 'travelling dress' that will make her appear to advantage at public events such as the races and when they visit large towns.

A travelling dress usually entailed a high-necked, long-sleeved dress covered with a relatively long jacket or coat. The one shown here is comfortable and elegant for a long carriage journey, which would have been draughty and disagreeable. Note that both costume, with its neck-protecting ruff, and description gesture to a fashion for Elizabeth Tudor, a monarch Catharine despises, as did Jane Austen.

FASHIONS

FOR

JANUARY, 1811

EXPLANATION OF THE PRINTS OF FASHION

NO. I – CARRIAGE DRESS

Gown of black Italian gauze worn over white, with long sleeves made high in the neck, with antique ruff *à-la-Queen Elizabeth*, ornamented round the bottom with a grey flossed silk trimming. A mantle of French grey satin, with collar fastened on the right shoulder with black brooch, and trimmed entirely round with a rich stamped velvet, lined with the same colour. A bonnet to correspond, with stamped velvet flower in front. Shoes of black or grey kid; gloves of the same.

Morning Carriage Dress

Extract from

CATHARINE, or THE BOWER

As her aunt prided herself on the exact propriety and neatness with which everything in her family was conducted, and had no higher satisfaction than that of knowing her house to be always in complete order, as her fortune was good, and her establishment ample, few were the preparations necessary for the reception of her visitors. The day of their arrival, so long expected, at length came, and the noise of the coach and four as it drove round the sweep was to Catharine a more interesting sound than the music of an Italian opera, which to most heroines is the height of enjoyment. Mr and Mrs Stanley were people of large fortune and high fashion. He was a member of the House of Commons, and they were therefore most agreeably necessitated to reside half the year in town; where Miss Stanley had been attended by the most capital masters from the time of her being six years old to the last spring, which comprehending a period of twelve years had been dedicated to the acquirement of accomplishments which were now to be displayed and in a few years entirely neglected.

She was not inelegant in her appearance, rather handsome, and naturally not deficient in abilities; but those years which ought to have been spent in the attainment of useful knowledge and mental improvement had been all bestowed in learning drawing, Italian and music, more especially the latter, and she now united to these accomplishments an understanding unimproved by reading and a mind totally devoid either of taste or judgement. Her temper was by nature good, but unassisted by reflection, she had neither patience under disappointment, nor could sacrifice her own inclinations to promote the happiness of others. All her ideas were towards the elegance of her appearance, the fashion of her dress, and the admiration she wished them to excite. She professed a love of books without reading, was lively without wit, and generally good humoured without merit.

Such was Camilla Stanley; and Catharine, who was prejudiced by her appearance, and who from her solitary situation was ready to like anyone, though her understanding and judgement would not otherwise have been easily satisfied, felt almost convinced when she saw her that Miss Stanley would be the very companion she wanted and in some degree make amends for the loss of Cecilia and Mary Wynne. She therefore attached herself to Camilla from the first day of her arrival, and from being the only young people in the house, they were by inclination constant companions. Kitty was herself a great reader, though perhaps not a very deep one, and felt therefore highly delighted to find that Miss Stanley was equally fond of it. Eager to know that their sentiments as to books were similar, she very soon began questioning her new acquaintance on the subject; but though she was well read in modern history herself, she chose rather to speak first of books of a lighter kind, of books universally read and admired.

'You have read Mrs Smith's novels, I suppose?' said she to her companion.

'Oh! yes,' replied the other, 'and I am quite delighted with them. They are the sweetest things in the world –'

'And which do you prefer of them?'

'Oh! dear, I think there is no comparison between them – *Emmeline* is *so much* better than any of the others –'

'Many people think so, I know; but there does not appear so great a disproportion in their merits to *me*; do you think it is better written?'

'Oh! I do not know anything about *that* – but it is better in *everything*. Besides, *Ethelinde* is so long –'

'That is a very common objection, I believe,' said Kitty, 'but for my own part, if a book is well written, I always find it too short.'

'So do I, only I get tired of it before it is finished.'

'But did not you find the story of *Ethelinde* very interesting? And the descriptions of Grasmere, are not they beautiful?'

'Oh! I missed them all, because I was in such a hurry to know the end of it –' Then from an easy transition she added, 'We are going to the Lakes this autumn, and I am quite mad with joy; Sir Henry Devereux has promised to go with us, and that will make it so pleasant, you know –'

'I dare say it will; but I think it is a pity that Sir Henry's powers of pleasing were not reserved for an occasion where they might be more wanted. However, I quite envy you the pleasure of such a scheme.'

'Oh! I am quite delighted with the thoughts of it; I can think of nothing else. I assure you I have done nothing for this last month but plan what clothes I should take with me, and I have at last determined to take very few indeed besides my travelling dress, and so I advise you to do, whenever you go; for I intend, in case we should fall in with any races, or stop at Matlock or Scarborough, to have some things made for the occasion.'

'You intend then to go into Yorkshire?'

'I believe not – indeed I know nothing of the route, for I never trouble myself about such things. I only know that we are to go from Derbyshire to Matlock and Scarborough, but to which of them first, I neither know nor care. I am in hopes of meeting some particular friends of mine at Scarborough. Augusta told me in her last letter that Sir Peter talked of going; but then you know that is so uncertain. I cannot bear Sir Peter, he is such a horrid creature –'

'He *is*, is he?' said Kitty, not knowing what else to say.

'Oh! he is quite shocking.'

Here the conversation was interrupted, and Kitty was left in a painful uncertainty as to the particulars of Sir Peter's character; she knew only that he was horrid and shocking, but why, and in what, yet remained to be discovered. She could scarcely resolve what to think of her new acquaintance; she appeared to be shamefully ignorant as to the geography of England, if she had understood her right, and equally devoid of taste and information. Kitty was, however, unwilling to decide hastily; she was at once desirous of doing Miss Stanley justice, and of having her own wishes in her answered; she determined therefore to suspend all judgement for some time.

THE MERRY WIDOW

On 2 November 1810, Princess Amelia died at the age of twenty-seven. *La Belle Assemblée* plunged itself into mourning paraphernalia, as did the country in general. Alongside the fashion illustration of 'second mourning evening dress', the November issue devoted its regular column, 'general observations on fashion and dress', exclusively to the topic of mourning dress.

The illustration recalls the flamboyant 'mourning' appearance of one of Jane Austen's most attractive villains, Lady Susan, in a work Austen began in her late teens and revised in 1805. Rather like Lady Susan herself, a shift is made to add allure to the severe edicts of mourning: no grey and only black could be worn and jewellery was expected to be in jet. Gold jewellery, white gloves and a grey silk shawl push at the boundaries of propriety. It may be that the journal had to swiftly customize an evening dress for the mourning issue.

We first see Lady Susan's duplicity, cunning and selfishness in a letter to her conspirator Alicia Johnson. It is followed by one penned by Catherine Vernon, virtuous and loyal wife to the brother of Susan's dead husband, in which she expresses to her mother Lady De Courcy her suspicions about Lady Susan's motives and behaviour in pressing to visit their country estate. Lady Susan brings a whole heap of trouble behind her seemingly demure widowly front.

FASHIONS

FOR

DECEMBER, 1810

EXPLANATION OF THE PRINTS OF FASHION
A SECOND MOURNING EVENING FULL DRESS

A white satin slip, ornamented round the bottom with gold, over which is worn a black patent net dress, with short sleeves. The dress entirely edged round with a rich joining lace, and ornamented with gold buttons; sloped up at the bottom in the front. Hair in curls divided up the forehead; necklace and earrings of gold; white kid gloves; shoes of white satin, with gold rosettes. A shawl of French grey silk, which is thrown across the shoulders in any way that occasion or fancy may dictate.

N.B. The Tarragona hat and dress represented in the plate, as a fashionable evening costume is the entire invention of Miss Blacklin, of New Bridge-street.

Evening Dress

Extract from

LADY SUSAN

Letter 2
LADY SUSAN VERNON TO MRS JOHNSON

❖ ❖ ❖

Langford

You were mistaken, my dear Alicia, in supposing me fixed at this place for the rest of the winter: it grieves me to say how greatly you were mistaken, for I have seldom spent three months more agreeably than those which have just flown away. At present, nothing goes smoothly; the females of the family are united against me. You foretold how it would be when I first came to Langford, and Mainwaring is so uncommonly pleasing that I was not without apprehensions for myself. I remember saying to myself, as I drove to the house, 'I like this man, pray heaven no harm come of it!' But I was determined to be discreet, to bear in mind my being only four months a widow, and to be as quiet as possible: and I have been so, my dear creature; I have admitted no one's attentions but Mainwaring's. I have avoided all general flirtation whatever; I have distinguished no creature besides, of all the numbers resorting hither, except Sir James Martin, on whom I bestowed a little notice, in order to detach him from Miss Mainwaring; but if the world could know my motive *there* they would honour me. I have been called an unkind mother, but it was the sacred impulse of maternal affection, it was the advantage of my daughter that led me on; and if that daughter were not the greatest simpleton on earth, I might have been rewarded for my exertions as I ought. Sir James did make proposals to me for Frederica; but Frederica, who was born to be the torment of my life, chose to set herself so violently against the match that I thought it better to lay aside the scheme for the present. I have more than once repented that I did not marry him myself; and were he but one degree less contemptibly weak I certainly should: but I must own myself rather romantic in that respect, and that riches only will not satisfy me. The event of all this is very provoking: Sir James is gone, Maria highly incensed, and Mrs Mainwaring insupportably jealous; so jealous, in short, and so enraged against me, that, in the fury of her temper, I should not be surprised at her appealing to her guardian, if she had the liberty of addressing him: but there your husband stands my friend; and the kindest, most amiable action of his life was his throwing her off for ever on her marriage. Keep up his resentment, therefore, I charge you. We are now in a sad state; no house was ever more altered; the whole party are at war, and Mainwaring scarcely dares speak to me. It is time for me to be gone; I have therefore determined on leaving them, and shall spend, I hope, a comfortable day with you in town within this week. If I am as little in favour with Mr Johnson as ever, you must come to me at 10 Wigmore Street; but I hope this may not be the case, for as Mr Johnson, with all his faults, is a man to whom that great word 'respectable' is always given, and I am known to be so intimate with his wife, his slighting me has an awkward look. I take London in on my way to that insupportable spot, a country village; for I am really going to Churchhill. Forgive me, my dear friend, it is my last resource. Were there another place in England open to me I would prefer it. Charles Vernon is my aversion; and I am afraid of his wife. At Churchhill, however, I must remain till I have something better in view. My young lady accompanies me to town, where I shall deposit her under the care of Miss Summers, in Wigmore Street, till she becomes a little more reasonable. She will make good connections there, as the girls are all of the best families. The price is immense, and much beyond what I can ever attempt to pay. Adieu, I will send you a line as soon as I arrive in town.

 Yours ever,
  S. Vernon

Letter 3
MRS VERNON TO LADY DE COURCY

Churchhill

My dear mother – I am very sorry to tell you that it will not be in our power to keep our promise of spending our Christmas with you; and we are prevented that happiness by a circumstance which is not likely to make us any amends. Lady Susan, in a letter to her brother-in-law, has declared her intention of visiting us almost immediately; and as such a visit is in all probability merely an affair of convenience, it is impossible to conjecture its length. I was by no means prepared for such an event, nor can I now account for her ladyship's conduct; Langford appeared so exactly the place for her in every respect, as well from the elegant and expensive style of living there as from her particular attachment to Mr Mainwaring, that I was very far from expecting so speedy a distinction, though I always imagined from her increasing friendship for us since her husband's death that we should, at some future period, be obliged to receive her. Mr Vernon, I think, was a great deal too kind to her when he was in Staffordshire; her behaviour to him, independent of her general character, has been so inexcusably artful and ungenerous since our marriage was first in agitation that no one less amiable and mild than himself could have overlooked it all; and though, as his brother's widow, and in narrow circumstances, it was proper to render her pecuniary assistance, I cannot help thinking his pressing invitation to her to visit us at Churchhill perfectly unnecessary. Disposed, however, as he always is to think the best of everyone, her display of grief, and professions of regret, and general resolutions of prudence, were sufficient to soften his heart and make him really confide in her sincerity; but, as for myself, I am still unconvinced, and plausibly as her ladyship has now written, I cannot make up my mind till I better understand her real meaning in coming to us. You may guess, therefore, my dear madam, with what feelings I look forward to her arrival. She will have occasion for all those attractive powers for which she is celebrated to gain any share of my regard; and I shall certainly endeavour to guard myself against their influence, if not accompanied by something more substantial. She expresses a most eager desire of being acquainted with me, and makes very gracious mention of my children but I am not quite weak enough to suppose a woman who has behaved with inattention, if not with unkindness, to her own child, should be attached to any of mine. Miss Vernon is to be placed at a school in London before her mother comes to us which I am glad of, for her sake and my own. It must be to her advantage to be separated from her mother, and a girl of sixteen who has received so wretched an education could not be a very desirable companion here. Reginald has long wished, I know, to see the captivating Lady Susan, and we shall depend on his joining our party soon.

I am glad to hear that my father continues so well; and am, with best love, &c.,

CATHERINE VERNON

TALKING MUSLIN

Jane Austen (probably) began to write a novel titled 'Susan' in 1798.

She most likely finished it the following year. A relatively frothy story about the adventures of a tomboyish country girl on a trip to bath with family friends was bought in 1803 but not published. It was finally published posthumously by another publisher in 1817 with the new title *Northanger Abbey*. The changing fortunes of this novel track those of one of its most famous talking points: muslin.

In the 1780s English East India companies started shipping this lightweight, very fine and breathable fabric – ideal for ballroom dancing – in bulk. It suited the emerging fashion for a higher-waisted 'round gown', where bodice and skirt are joined to make a single garment. Henry Tilney is pleased to have purchased 'a true Indian muslin' at a good price and just like Eleanor Tilney, Henry's sister, the Austen women planned their use of muslin carefully. In a letter to Cassandra of 25 January 1801, Jane instructs her sister to ensure she buy a longer length of muslin for Jane's gown due to Jane's unusual height.

The 1808 illustration suggests Catherine's 'muslin robe with blue trimmings'. The freshness of the costume and its wearer, who earnestly consults her dance card, captures Austen's treatment of a young heroine in this scene of her first ball in Bath Assembly Rooms.

FASHIONS

FOR

AUGUST, 1808

EXPLANATION OF THE PRINTS OF FASHION

ENGLISH COSTUME – NO. 3

A round robe of India muslin, Paris net, or leno, worn over a white sarsnet, or cambric slip; tamboured in a snail stripe, either in white or colours. The dress formed on the most simple construction; a plain back, and wrap front, sitting close to the form; a plain frock sleeve, edged with the antique scollop; a short train, finished round the bottom in a similar style. Hair brought tight from the roots behind, and twisted in a cable knot on one side, the ends formed in falling ringlets on the other; with full irregular curls. A full red and white rose, or ranunculus, placed on the crown of the head, rather towards one side. Emerald necklace linked with dead gold. Ear-rings and bracelets to correspond. French kid gloves above the elbow. Pea-green slippers of fancy kid.

London Evening Dress

Extract from

NORTHANGER ABBEY

Every morning now brought its regular duties – shops were to be visited; some new part of the town to be looked at; and the Pump-room to be attended, where they paraded up and down for an hour, looking at everybody and speaking to no one. The wish of a numerous acquaintance in Bath was still uppermost with Mrs Allen, and she repeated it after every fresh proof, which every morning brought, of her knowing nobody at all.

They made their appearance in the Lower Rooms; and here fortune was more favourable to our heroine. The master of the ceremonies introduced to her a very gentlemanlike young man as a partner; his name was Tilney. He seemed to be about four or five and twenty, was rather tall, had a pleasing countenance, a very intelligent and lively eye, and, if not quite handsome, was very near it. His address was good, and Catherine felt herself in high luck. There was little leisure for speaking while they danced; but when they were seated at tea, she found him as agreeable as she had already given him credit for being. He talked with fluency and spirit – and there was an archness and pleasantry in his manner which interested, though it was hardly understood by her. After chatting some time on such matters as naturally arose from the objects around them, he suddenly addressed her with – 'I have hitherto been very remiss, madam, in the proper attentions of a partner here; I have not yet asked you how long you have been in Bath; whether you were ever here before; whether you have been at the Upper Rooms, the theatre, and the concert; and how you like the place altogether. I have been very negligent – but are you now at leisure to satisfy me in these particulars? If you are I will begin directly.'

'You need not give yourself that trouble, sir.'

'No trouble, I assure you, madam.' Then forming his features into a set smile, and affectedly softening his voice, he added, with a simpering air, 'Have you been long in Bath, madam?'

'About a week, sir,' replied Catherine, trying not to laugh.

'Really!' with affected astonishment.

'Why should you be surprised, sir?'

'Why, indeed!' said he, in his natural tone. 'But some emotion must appear to be raised by your reply, and surprise is more easily assumed, and not less reasonable than any other. Now let us go on. Were you never here before, madam?'

'Never, sir.'

'Indeed! Have you yet honoured the Upper Rooms?'

'Yes, sir, I was there last Monday.'

'Have you been to the theatre?'

'Yes, sir, I was at the play on Tuesday.'

'To the concert?'

'Yes, sir, on Wednesday.'

'And are you altogether pleased with Bath?'

'Yes – I like it very well.'

'Now I must give one smirk, and then we may be rational again.' Catherine turned away her head, not knowing whether she might venture to laugh. 'I see what you think of me,' said he gravely – 'I shall make but a poor figure in your journal tomorrow.'

'My journal!'

'Yes, I know exactly what you will say: Friday, went to the Lower Rooms; wore my sprigged muslin robe with blue trimmings – plain black shoes – appeared to much advantage; but was strangely harassed by a queer, half-witted man, who would make me dance with him, and distressed me by his nonsense.'

'Indeed I shall say no such thing.'

'Shall I tell you what you ought to say?'

'If you please.'

'I danced with a very agreeable young man, introduced by Mr King; had a great deal of conversation with him – seems a most extraordinary genius – hope I may know more of him. *That*, madam, is what I *wish* you to say.'

'But, perhaps, I keep no journal.'

'Perhaps you are not sitting in this room, and I am not sitting by you. These are points in which a doubt is equally possible. Not keep a journal! How are your absent cousins to understand the tenor of your life in Bath without one? How are the civilities and compliments of every day to be related as they ought to be, unless noted down every evening in a journal? How are your various dresses to be remembered, and the particular state of your complexion, and curl of your hair to be described in all their diversities, without having constant recourse to a journal? My dear madam, I am not so ignorant of young ladies' ways as you wish to believe me; it is this delightful habit of journalising which largely contributes to form the easy style of writing for which ladies are so generally celebrated. Everybody allows that the talent of writing agreeable letters is peculiarly female. Nature may have done something, but I am sure it must be essentially assisted by the practice of keeping a journal.'

'I have sometimes thought,' said Catherine, doubtingly,

'whether ladies do write so much better letters than gentlemen! That is – I should not think the superiority was always on our side.'

'As far as I have had opportunity of judging, it appears to me that the usual style of letter-writing among women is faultless, except in three particulars.'

'And what are they?'

'A general deficiency of subject, a total inattention to stops, and a very frequent ignorance of grammar.'

'Upon my word! I need not have been afraid of disclaiming the compliment. You do not think too highly of us in that way.'

'I should no more lay it down as a general rule that women write better letters than men, than that they sing better duets, or draw better landscapes. In every power, of which taste is the foundation, excellence is pretty fairly divided between the sexes.'

They were interrupted by Mrs Allen: 'My dear Catherine,' said she, 'do take this pin out of my sleeve; I am afraid it has torn a hole already; I shall be quite sorry if it has, for this is a favourite gown, though it cost but nine shillings a yard.'

'That is exactly what I should have guessed it, madam,' said Mr Tilney, looking at the muslin.

'Do you understand muslins, sir?'

'Particularly well; I always buy my own cravats, and am allowed to be an excellent judge; and my sister has often trusted me in the choice of a gown. I bought one for her the other day, and it was pronounced to be a prodigious bargain by every lady who saw it. I gave but five shillings a yard for it, and a true Indian muslin.'

Mrs Allen was quite struck by his genius. 'Men commonly take so little notice of those things,' said she; 'I can never get

Mr Allen to know one of my gowns from another. You must be a great comfort to your sister, sir.'

'I hope I am, madam.'

'And pray, sir, what do you think of Miss Morland's gown?'

'It is very pretty, madam,' said he, gravely examining it; 'but I do not think it will wash well; I am afraid it will fray.'

'How can you,' said Catherine, laughing, 'be so –' She had almost said 'strange'.

'I am quite of your opinion, sir,' replied Mrs Allen; 'and so I told Miss Morland when she bought it.'

'But then you know, madam, muslin always turns to some account or other; Miss Morland will get enough out of it for a handkerchief, or a cap, or a cloak. Muslin can never be said to be wasted. I have heard my sister say so forty times, when she has been extravagant in buying more than she wanted, or careless in cutting it to pieces.'

'Bath is a charming place, sir; there are so many good shops here. We are sadly off in the country; not but what we have very good shops in Salisbury, but it is so far to go – eight miles is a long way; Mr Allen says it is nine, measured nine; but I am sure it cannot be more than eight; and it is such a fag – I come back tired to death. Now, here one can step out of doors and get a thing in five minutes.'

Mr Tilney was polite enough to seem interested in what she said; and she kept him on the subject of muslins till the dancing recommenced. Catherine feared, as she listened to their discourse, that he indulged himself a little too much with the foibles of others. 'What are you thinking of so earnestly?' said he, as they walked back to the ballroom; 'not of your partner, I hope, for, by that shake of the head, your meditations are not satisfactory.'

Catherine coloured, and said, 'I was not thinking of anything.'

'That is artful and deep, to be sure; but I had rather be told at once that you will not tell me.'

'Well then, I will not.'

'Thank you; for now we shall soon be acquainted, as I am authorised to tease you on this subject whenever we meet, and nothing in the world advances intimacy so much.'

They danced again; and, when the assembly closed, parted, on the lady's side at least, with a strong inclination for continuing the acquaintance. Whether she thought of him so much, while she drank her warm wine and water, and prepared herself for bed, as to dream of him when there, cannot be ascertained.

BOYS AND BONNETS

CATHERINE MORLAND IN *NORTHANGER ABBEY* HAS YET TO HAVE HER EYES OPENED TO THE SELFISH CUNNING OF HER NEW BATH FRIEND, ISABELLA THORPE. IN THIS PASSAGE, ISABELLA SEEKS TO COMBINE HER DESIRE TO SHOW OFF THE LATEST HAT SHE HAS HER EYE ON WITH THE PURSUIT OF TWO YOUNG MEN WHO HAVE BEEN EYEING THEM UP IN THE PUMP ROOM.

Women could peek out of or throw a glance from a bonnet, or use it to shade their blushes. An interest in bonnets was not a subterfuge for Jane Austen as it is for Isabella; she comments frequently and with expertise on headwear in her correspondence. The only portrait we know to be of her, by her sister Cassandra, dating from around 1804, is from behind with her head and face concealed by a large blue 'bag' bonnet.

Female walking-dress always required a hat. In this illustration, a fur hat and a melon bonnet (referring to the shape which resembles the fruit) provide warmth and protection from wind: the Bath social season ran from late September to mid-December so warm outdoor-wear was required. The two women in this illustration are not, as Isabella suggests, wearing exactly the same to gain 'notice' from men, but they are in eye-catching complementary red and 'American' green (a light apple-green).

FASHIONS

FOR

JANUARY, 1808

EXPLANATION OF THE PRINTS OF FASHION

NO. I – A MORNING DRESS

A round cambric gown, a walking length, with short full sleeve, and puckered cuff, buttoned or laced down the back, and made high round the neck, with a full frill of lace. A military stock, edged round the chin with the same. A figured Chinese scarf, the colour American green, twisted round the figure in the style of antique drapery. Melon bonnet the same colour, striped, and trimmed to correspond with the scarf. Hair in irregular curls on the forehead. Earrings of gold or topaz. Long York tan, or Limerick gloves, above the elbows. Slippers of yellow Morocco. This dress, divested of the bonnet, is considered genteel *neglige* for any period of the day.

NO. 2 – A MORNING WALKING, OR CARRIAGE, HABILIMENT

A simple breakfast robe of Indian muslin, or cambric; with plain high collar, and long sleeve. Plain chemisette front, buttoned down the bosom. A Calypso wrap of marone velvet, or kerseymere, trimmed entirely round with white ermine, or swansdown. Spanish hanging-sleeve, suspended from the back, and falling over the left shoulder, terminating in a round point below the elbow. The ornament is lined throughout with skin the same as the trimming. A mountain hat of white imperial beaver, or fur, tied under the chin with a ribband the colour of the coat. Gloves and shoes of American green, or buff. Cropt hair, confined with a band, and curled over the left eye.

Fashionable Walking Dresses

Extract from
NORTHANGER ABBEY

'But, my dearest Catherine, have you settled what to wear on your head tonight? I am determined at all events to be dressed exactly like you. The men take notice of *that* sometimes, you know.'

'But it does not signify if they do,' said Catherine, very innocently.

'Signify! Oh, heavens! I make it a rule never to mind what they say. They are very often amazingly impertinent if you do not treat them with spirit, and make them keep their distance.'

'Are they? Well, I never observed *that*. They always behave very well to me.'

'Oh! They give themselves such airs. They are the most conceited creatures in the world, and think themselves of so much importance! By the by, though I have thought of it a hundred times, I have always forgot to ask you what is your favourite complexion in a man. Do you like them best dark or fair?'

'I hardly know. I never much thought about it. Something between both, I think. Brown – not fair, and – and not very dark.'

'Very well, Catherine. That is exactly he. I have not forgot your description of Mr Tilney – "a brown skin, with dark eyes, and rather dark hair". Well, my taste is different. I prefer light eyes, and as to complexion – do you know – I like a sallow better than any other. You must not betray me, if you should ever meet with one of your acquaintance answering that description.'

'Betray you! What do you mean?'

'Nay, do not distress me. I believe I have said too much. Let us drop the subject.'

Catherine, in some amazement, complied, and after remaining a few moments silent, was on the point of reverting to what interested her at that time rather more than anything else in the world, Laurentina's skeleton, when her friend prevented her, by saying, 'For heaven's sake! Let us move away from this end of the room. Do you know, there are two odious young men who have been staring at me this half-hour. They really put me quite out of countenance. Let us go and look at the arrivals. They will hardly follow us there.'

Away they walked to the book; and while Isabella examined the names, it was Catherine's employment to watch the proceedings of these alarming young men.

'They are not coming this way, are they? I hope they are not so impertinent as to follow us. Pray let me know if they are coming. I am determined I will not look up.'

In a few moments Catherine, with unaffected pleasure, assured her that she need not be longer uneasy, as the gentlemen had just left the Pump-room.

'And which way are they gone?' said Isabella, turning hastily round. 'One was a very good-looking young man.'

'They went towards the churchyard.'

'Well, I am amazingly glad I have got rid of them! And now, what say you to going to Edgar's Buildings with me, and looking at my new hat? You said you should like to see it.'

Catherine readily agreed. 'Only,' she added, 'perhaps we may overtake the two young men.'

'Oh! Never mind that. If we make haste, we shall pass by them presently, and I am dying to show you my hat.'

'But if we only wait a few minutes, there will be no danger of our seeing them at all.'

'I shall not pay them any such compliment, I assure you. I have no notion of treating men with such respect. *That* is the way to spoil them.'

Catherine had nothing to oppose against such reasoning; and therefore, to show the independence of Miss Thorpe, and her resolution of humbling the sex, they set off immediately as fast as they could walk, in pursuit of the two young men.

Half a minute conducted them through the Pumpyard to the archway, opposite Union Passage; but here they were stopped. Everybody acquainted with Bath may remember the difficulties of crossing Cheap Street at this point; it is indeed a street of so impertinent a nature, so unfortunately connected with the great London and Oxford roads, and the principal inn of the city, that a day never passes in which parties of ladies, however important their business, whether in quest of pastry, millinery, or even (as in the present case) of young men, are not detained on one side or other by carriages, horsemen, or carts. This evil had been felt and lamented, at least three times a day, by Isabella since her residence in Bath; and she was now fated to feel and lament it once more, for at the very moment of coming opposite to Union Passage, and within view of the two gentlemen who were proceeding through the crowds, and threading the gutters of that interesting alley, they were prevented crossing by the approach of a gig, driven along on bad pavement by a most knowing-looking coachman with all the vehemence that could most fitly endanger the lives of himself, his companion, and his horse.

'Oh, these odious gigs!' said Isabella, looking up. 'How I detest them.' But this detestation, though so just, was of short duration, for she looked again and exclaimed, 'Delightful! Mr Morland and my brother!'

'Good heaven! 'Tis James!' was uttered at the same moment by Catherine; and, on catching the young men's eyes, the horse was immediately checked with a violence which almost threw him on his haunches, and the servant having now scampered up, the gentlemen jumped out, and the equipage was delivered to his care.

Catherine, by whom this meeting was wholly unexpected, received her brother with the liveliest pleasure; and he, being of a very amiable disposition, and sincerely attached to her, gave every proof on his side of equal satisfaction, which he could have leisure to do, while the bright eyes of Miss Thorpe were incessantly challenging his notice; and to her his *devoirs* were speedily paid, with a mixture of joy and embarrassment which might have informed Catherine, had she been more expert in the development of other people's feelings, and less simply engrossed by her own, that her brother thought her friend quite as pretty as she could do herself.

A GRACIOUS DANCE

BALLS OFTEN TEST THE VIRTUE AND VALOUR OF AUSTEN'S HEROINES. EMMA WATSON IS NO EXCEPTION IN THIS SCENE FROM THE UNFINISHED WORK IN A (ROUGH) MANUSCRIPT DRAFT KNOWN AS *THE WATSONS*. JANE AUSTEN LIKELY BEGAN COMPOSING THIS WHILE SHE WAS LIVING IN BATH IN 1804 BUT ABANDONED IT ON THE DEATH OF HER FATHER IN JANUARY 1805.

Emma attracts attention at a small-town assembly in Surrey which is attended by attractive army officers and the local gentry of Osborne Castle. Emma takes pity on ten-year-old Charles Blake, observing the little boy's bitter disappointment when Miss Osborne reneges on her promise to dance the first two dances with him.

The *Belle Assemblée* evening dress ensemble is carefully accessorized and the whole points to cosmopolitan taste: a *ridicule aux getons* (a small handbag or 'reticule' in which to store tokens), a Sicilian tunic and earrings of a Maltese fashion, pearl trims and jewellery. It is completed by the all-important gloves – here of white kid, the preferred material for women – worn over the elbow for evening wear. One arm is elegantly extended to accept a dance or make a greeting. Charles is 'provided with his gloves and charged to keep them on', which was essential for propriety.

FASHIONS

FOR

FEBRUARY, 1812

EXPLANATION OF THE PRINTS OF FASHION

NO. I – EVENING COSTUME

An amber crape dress over white sarsnet, trimmed with pearls or white beads, with a demi-train; a light short jacket, rather scanty, with two separate fancy folds, depending about three quarters down the front of the skirt, forming in appearance a kind of Sicilian tunic, and trimmed down each division, like the bottom of the dress, with a single row of pearls: short sleeves, not very high above the elbow, fitting close to the arm, and ornamented at the top with distinct points of satin, the same colour as the dress, relieved by pearls; two rows of the same costly material or of beads, according as the robe is ornamented, form a girdle. The hair dressed in the antique Roman style, with tresses brought together and confined at the back of the head, terminating either in ringlets or in two light knots; a braid of plaited hair drawn over a demi-turban formed of plain amber satin, with an elegantly embroidered stripe of white satin, separated by rows of pearl, and a superb sprig of pearls in front. Necklace of one single row of large pearls, with earrings of the Maltese fashion to correspond. *Ridicule aux getons* of slate colour, shot with pink; the firm base secured by a cover of pink stamped velvet, with pink tassels. Italian slippers of amber, fringed with silver, or ornamented round the ankle with a row of pearls or beads.

White kid gloves.—This elegant dress owes its invention to the tasteful fancy of Mrs. Schabner, of Tavistock-street.

Evening Dress

Extract from

THE WATSONS

Emma, in the meanwhile, was not unobserved or unadmired herself. A new face, and a very pretty one, could not be slighted. Her name was whispered from one party to another; and no sooner had the signal been given by the orchestra's striking up a favourite air, which seemed to call the young to their duty and people the centre of the room, than she found herself engaged to dance with a brother officer, introduced by Captain Hunter.

Emma Watson was not more than of the middle height, well made and plump, with an air of healthy vigour. Her skin was very brown, but clear, smooth, and glowing, which, with a lively eye, a sweet smile, and an open countenance, gave beauty to attract and expression to make that beauty improve on acquaintance. Having no reason to be dissatisfied with her partner, the evening began very pleasantly to her, and her feelings perfectly coincided with the reiterated observation of others, that it was an excellent ball. The two first dances were not quite over when the returning sound of carriages after a long interruption called general notice, and 'The Osbornes are coming! The Osbornes are coming!' was repeated round the room. After some minutes of extraordinary bustle without and watchful curiosity within, the important party, preceded by the attentive master of the inn to open a door which was never shut, made their appearance. They consisted of Lady Osborne; her son, Lord Osborne; her daughter, Miss Osborne; Miss Carr, her daughter's friend; Mr Howard, formerly tutor to Lord Osborne, now clergyman of the parish in which the castle stood; Mrs Blake, a widow sister who lived with him; her son, a fine boy of ten years old; and Mr Tom Musgrave, who probably, imprisoned within his own room, had been listening in bitter impatience to the sound of the music for the last half-hour. In their progress up the room, they paused almost immediately behind Emma to receive the compliments of some acquaintance; and she heard Lady Osborne observe that they had made a point of coming early for the gratification of Mrs Blake's little boy, who was uncommonly fond of dancing. Emma looked at them all as they passed, but chiefly and with most interest on Tom Musgrave, who was certainly a genteel, good-looking young man. Of the females, Lady Osborne had by much the finest person; though nearly fifty, she was very handsome, and had all the dignity of rank.

Lord Osborne was a very fine young man; but there was an air of coldness, of carelessness, even of awkwardness about him, which seemed to speak him out of his element in a ballroom. He came, in fact, only because it was judged expedient for him to please the borough; he was not fond of women's company, and he never danced. Mr Howard was an agreeable-looking man, a little more than thirty.

At the conclusion of the two dances, Emma found herself, she knew not how, seated among the Osborne set; and she was immediately struck with the fine countenance and animated gestures of the little boy, as he was standing before his mother, wondering when they should begin.

'You will not be surprised at Charles's impatience,' said Mrs Blake, a lively, pleasant-looking little woman of five- or six-and-thirty, to a lady who was standing near her, 'when you know what a partner he is to have. Miss Osborne has been so very kind as to promise to dance the two first dances with him.'

'Oh, yes! we have been engaged this week,' cried the boy, 'and we are to dance down every couple.'

On the other side of Emma, Miss Osborne, Miss Carr, and a party of young men were standing engaged in very lively consultation; and soon afterwards she saw the smartest officer of the set walking off to the orchestra to order the dance, while Miss Osborne, passing before her to her little expecting partner, hastily said: 'Charles, I beg your pardon for not keeping my engagement, but I am going to dance these two dances with Colonel Beresford. I know you will excuse me, and I will certainly dance with you after tea'; and without staying for an answer, she turned again to Miss Carr, and in another minute was led by Colonel Beresford to begin the set. If the poor little boy's face had in its happiness been interesting to Emma, it was infinitely more so under this sudden reverse; he stood the picture of disappointment, with crimsoned cheeks, quivering lips, and eyes bent on the floor. His mother, stifling her own mortification, tried to soothe his with the prospect of Miss Osborne's second promise; but though he contrived to utter, with an effort of boyish bravery, 'Oh, I do not mind it!' it was very evident, by the unceasing agitation of his features, that he minded it as much as ever.

Emma did not think or reflect; she felt and acted. 'I shall be very happy to dance with you, sir, if you like it,' said she, holding out her hand with the most unaffected good-humour. The boy, in one moment restored to all his first delight, looked joyfully at his mother; and stepping forwards with an honest and simple, 'Thank you, ma'am,' was instantly ready to attend his new acquaintance. The thankfulness of Mrs Blake was more diffuse; with a look most expressive of unexpected pleasure and lively gratitude, she turned to her neighbour with repeated and fervent acknowledgements of so great and condescending a kindness to her boy. Emma, with perfect truth, could assure her that she could not be giving greater pleasure than she felt herself; and Charles being provided with his gloves and charged to keep them on, they joined the set which was now rapidly forming, with nearly equal complacency. It was a partnership which could not be noticed without surprise. It gained her a broad stare from Miss Osborne and Miss Carr as they passed her in the dance. 'Upon my word, Charles, you are in luck,' said the former, as she turned him; 'you have got a better partner than me'; to which the happy Charles answered, 'Yes.'

CHILDREN FIRST

When Jane Austen received proofs of her first novel, *Sense and Sensibility* (1811), she commented to her sister in a letter of 25 April, 'I can no more forget it than a mother can forget her sucking child'.

In this scene from the novel, the three impoverished Dashwood sisters and their widowed mother have moved to Barton Cottage in Devon, which belongs to relative and neighbour Sir John Middleton. When Lady Middleton comes to visit, the presence of her young son eases the awkwardness. The novel is much preoccupied with sibling relationships and the dangers of favouring particular children over others.

La Belle Assemblée rarely included children in its fashion illustrations: here, one of two fashionable women meeting at Hyde Park with a small child peeking from the skirts of his mother gives us some insight into what boys of about the same age and wealth as the small Middleton wore. In the 1780s parents began to put boys above the age of four in trousers and, like a mini grown-up, he also sports a fine fur hat with a jaunty feather. But he retains the back-fastening 'frock' worn by children and a front-fastening loose coat ('wrapping coat'), here in a handsome cashmere. Childhood here and in the novel is represented as both part of and apart from polite sociable discourse.

FASHIONS

FOR

MAY, 1808

EXPLANATION OF THE PRINTS OF FASHION

ENGLISH COSTUME

NO. I – A WALKING DRESS

A plain muslin walking dress, with Spanish spencer of celestial blue, or shaded lilac sarsnet, ornamented entirely round with the new Chinese trimming, and confined round the waist with a large cord, and tassels to correspond. A bonnet composed of the same materials as the spencer, with *tiara* front, and Chinese trimming. Shoes of pale blue, or lilac kid. Gloves of York tan.

NO. 2. – A LADY AND CHILD

A high gown of French cambric, with long sleeves, shirt front, and frill of scalloped lace. A French hanging sleeve; coat with slashed skirt, and Spanish lappells, formed of figured Imperial sarsnet or Chinese silk – its colour spring green, buff, or jonquille, ornamented with a floss silk trimming of agreeably contrasted shades. A Gipsy hat of straw, or figured Imperial chip, worn rather forward; a little French cap appearing beneath, and the hair formed in close curls, or a waved crop behind. The hat tied simply across the crown with a narrow white ribband. A nankeen slipper, or shoe of pale green kid. Gloves of pale Limerick.

CHILD'S ATTIRE – A frock, and short trowsers of cambric, with Turkish pomposas of jonquille kid. A wrapping coat with deep cape, formed of fine scarlet, or purple kerseymere. A beaver hat and feather of pale brown, or dove colour.

Hyde Park Walking Dresses

Extract from

SENSE AND SENSIBILITY

The situation of the house was good. High hills rose immediately behind, and at no great distance on each side; some of which were open downs, the others cultivated and woody. The village of Barton was chiefly on one of these hills, and formed a pleasant view from the cottage windows. The prospect in front was more extensive; it commanded the whole of the valley, and reached into the country beyond. The hills which surrounded the cottage terminated the valley in that direction; under another name, and in another course, it branched out again between two of the steepest of them.

With the size and furniture of the house Mrs Dashwood was upon the whole well satisfied; for though her former style of life rendered many additions to the latter indispensable, yet to add and improve was a delight to her; and she had at this time ready money enough to supply all that was wanted of greater elegance to the apartments. 'As for the house itself, to be sure,' said she, 'it is too small for our family, but we will make ourselves tolerably comfortable for the present, as it is too late in the year for improvements. Perhaps in the spring, if I have plenty of money, as I dare say I shall, we may think about building. These parlours are both too small for such parties of our friends as I hope to see often collected here; and I have some thoughts of throwing the passage into one of them with perhaps a part of the other, and so leave the remainder of that other for an entrance; this, with a new drawing-room which may be easily added, and a bedchamber and garret above, will make it a very snug little cottage. I could wish the stairs were handsome. But one must not expect everything; though I suppose it would be no difficult matter to widen them. I shall see how much I am beforehand with the world in the spring, and we will plan our improvements accordingly.'

In the meantime, till all these alterations could be made from the savings of an income of five hundred a year by a woman who never saved in her life, they were wise enough to be contented with the house as it was; and each of them was busy in arranging their particular concerns, and endeavouring, by placing around them their books and other possessions, to form themselves a home. Marianne's pianoforte was unpacked and properly disposed of; and Elinor's drawings were affixed to the walls of their sitting-room.

In such employments as these they were interrupted soon after breakfast the next day by the entrance of their landlord, who called to welcome them to Barton, and to offer them every accommodation from his own house and garden in which theirs might at present be deficient. Sir John Middleton was a good-looking man about forty. He had formerly visited at Stanhill, but it was too long ago for his young cousins to remember him. His countenance was thoroughly good-humoured; and his manners were as friendly as the style of his letter. Their arrival seemed to afford him real satisfaction, and their comfort to be an object of real solicitude to him. He said much of his earnest desire of their living in the most sociable terms with his family, and pressed them so cordially to dine at Barton Park every day till they were better settled at home, that, though his entreaties were carried to a point of perseverance beyond civility, they could not give offence. His kindness was not confined to words; for within an hour after he left them, a large basket full of garden stuff and fruit arrived from the park, which was followed before the end of the day by a present of game. He insisted moreover on conveying all their letters to and from the post for them, and would not be denied the satisfaction of sending them his newspaper every day.

Lady Middleton had sent a very civil message by him, denoting her intention of waiting on Mrs Dashwood as soon as she could be assured that her visit would be no inconvenience; and as this message was answered by an invitation equally polite, her ladyship was introduced to them the next day.

They were of course very anxious to see a person on whom so much of their comfort at Barton must depend; and the elegance of her appearance was favourable to their wishes. Lady Middleton was not more than six or seven and twenty; her face was handsome, her figure tall and striking, and her address graceful. Her manners had all the elegance which her husband's wanted. But they would have been improved by some share of his frankness and warmth; and her visit was long enough to detract something from their first admiration, by showing that though perfectly well-bred, she was reserved, cold, and had nothing to say for herself beyond the most commonplace enquiry or remark.

Conversation however was not wanted, for Sir John was very chatty, and Lady Middleton had taken the wise precaution of bringing with her their eldest child, a fine little boy about six years old, by which means there was one subject always to be recurred to by the ladies in case of extremity, for they had to enquire his name and age, admire his beauty, and ask him questions which his mother answered for him, while he hung about her and held down his head, to the great surprise of her ladyship, who wondered at his being so shy before company as he could make noise enough at home. On every formal visit a child ought to be of the party, by way of provision for discourse. In the present case it took up ten minutes to determine whether the boy were most like his father or mother, and in what particular he resembled either, for of course everybody differed, and everybody was astonished at the opinion of the others.

An opportunity was soon to be given to the Dashwoods of debating on the rest of the children, as Sir John would not leave the house without securing their promise of dining at the park the next day.

KENSINGTON GARDENS

JANE AUSTEN MENTIONS IN A LETTER OF 25 APRIL 1811 THAT SHE HAD ENJOYED A WALK IN FASHIONABLE KENSINGTON GARDENS IN LONDON WITH HER BROTHER HENRY AND FRIENDS. ON A FINE SUNDAY IN MARCH, ELINOR DASHWOOD WALKS IN THE SAME GARDENS WITH HER HOST MRS JENNINGS.

The secret engagement of vulgar, ambitious Lucy Steele to Edward Ferrars, the object of Elinor's affection, has recently come to light. They meet Anne, Lucy's older sister, who cannot wait to impart the details. Like so many of Austen's silly speakers, Anne exposes her own failings, especially in her references to clothing and accessories: a desperate attempt to attract the doctor she so admires by donning a pair of silk stockings and pink hat ribbons, vanity in worrying about her own sister Lucy's refusal to prettify Anne's bonnets, and spite by expressing concern that Elinor's muslin might tear. Austen comments in a letter of 24 December 1798 that she plans to turn the 'coarse spot' muslin that she is 'libelled' for owning into a petticoat.

One of the ladies pictured here is clad in a richly embroidered muslin of the more expensive 'India' origin. She looks away and appears, like Elinor, to be seeking to establish some distance from her seated companion who is dressed in full 'village' splendour.

FASHIONS

FOR

AUGUST, 1807

EXPLANATION OF THE PRINTS OF FASHION

ENGLISH COSTUME

KENSINGTON-GARDEN DRESSES

No. 1 – A plain cambric round dress, a walking length. Roman spencer of celestial blue sarsnet, with Vandyke lappels and falling collar; finished with the same round the bottom of the waist, and flowing open in front of the bosom. A village hat of Imperial chip, with bee-hive crown, confined under the chin with ribbon the colour of the spencer. Cropped hair, divided in the centre of the forehead with full curls. Gloves and shoes of lemon-coloured kid. Parasol of salmon-coloured sarsnet.

No. 2 – Round train dress of India muslin, with short sleeves, ornamented round the bottom and sleeves with a rich border of needle-work. Promenade tippet of Brussels lace, lined with white satin. Hat of white chip, or fancy cap of lilac satin, with a Brussels lace veil. Hair confined in braids over the right temple, and formed in loose curls on the opposite side. Gold hoop earrings. Gloves and slippers of lilac kid.

Kensington Garden Dresses

Extract from

SENSE AND SENSIBILITY

The third day succeeding their knowledge of the particulars, was so fine, so beautiful a Sunday as to draw many to Kensington Gardens, though it was only the second week in March. Mrs Jennings and Elinor were of the number; but Marianne, who knew that the Willoughbys were again in town, and had a constant dread of meeting them, chose rather to stay at home, than venture into so public a place.

An intimate acquaintance of Mrs Jennings joined them soon after they entered the Gardens, and Elinor was not sorry that by her continuing with them, and engaging all Mrs Jennings's conversation, she was herself left to quiet reflection. She saw nothing of the Willoughbys, nothing of Edward, and for some time nothing of anybody who could by any chance whether grave or gay, be interesting to her. But at last she found herself with some surprise, accosted by Miss Steele, who, though looking rather shy, expressed great satisfaction in meeting them, and on receiving encouragement from the particular kindness of Mrs Jennings, left her own party for a short time, to join theirs. Mrs Jennings immediately whispered to Elinor, 'Get it all out of her, my dear. She will tell you anything if you ask. You see I cannot leave Mrs Clarke.'

It was lucky, however, for Mrs Jennings's curiosity and

Elinor's too, that she would tell anything *without* being asked, for nothing would otherwise have been learnt.

'I am so glad to meet you,' said Miss Steele, taking her familiarly by the arm – 'for I wanted to see you of all things in the world.' And then lowering her voice, 'I suppose Mrs Jennings has heard all about it. Is she angry?'

'Not at all, I believe, with you.'

'That is a good thing. And Lady Middleton, is *she* angry?'

'I cannot suppose it possible that she should.'

'I am monstrous glad of it. Good gracious! I have had such a time of it! I never saw Lucy in such a rage in my life. She vowed at first she would never trim me up a new bonnet, nor do anything else for me again, so long as she lived; but now she is quite come to, and we are as good friends as ever. Look, she made me this bow to my hat, and put in the feather last night. There now, *you* are going to laugh at me too. But why should not I wear pink ribbons? I do not care if it *is* the Doctor's favourite colour. I am sure, for my part, I should never have known he *did* like it better than any other colour, if he had not happened to say so. My cousins have been so plaguing me! I declare sometimes I do not know which way to look before them.'

She had wandered away to a subject on which Elinor had nothing to say, and therefore soon judged it expedient to find her way back again to the first.

'Well, but Miss Dashwood,' speaking triumphantly, 'people may say what they choose about Mr Ferrars's declaring he would not have Lucy, for it's no such a thing I can tell you; and it's quite a shame for such ill natured reports to be spread abroad. Whatever Lucy might think about it herself, you know, it was no business of other people to set it down for certain.'

'I never heard anything of the kind hinted at before, I assure you,' said Elinor.

'Oh! did not you? But it *was* said, I know, very well, and by more than one; for Miss Godby told Miss Sparks, that nobody in their senses could expect Mr Ferrars to give up a woman like Miss Morton, with thirty thousand pounds to her fortune, for Lucy Steele that had nothing at all; and I had it from Miss Sparks myself. And besides that, my cousin Richard said himself, that when it came to the point, he was afraid Mr Ferrars would be off; and when Edward did not come near us for three days, I could not tell what to think myself; and I believe in my heart Lucy gave it all up for lost; for we came away from your brother's on Wednesday, and we saw nothing of him not all Thursday, Friday, and Saturday, and did not know what was become with him. Once Lucy thought to write to him, but then her spirit rose against that. However this morning he came just as we came home from church; and then it all came out, how he had been sent for Wednesday to Harley Street, and been talked to by his mother and all of them, and how he had declared before them all that he loved nobody but Lucy, and nobody but Lucy would he have. And how he had been so worried by what passed, that as soon as he had went away from his mother's house, he had got upon his horse, and rid into the country somewhere or other; and how he had staid about at an inn all Thursday and Friday, on purpose to get the better of it. And after thinking it all over and over again, he said, it seemed to him as if, now he had no fortune, and no nothing at all, it would be quite unkind to keep her on to the engagement, because it must be for her loss, for he had nothing but two thousand pounds, and no hope of anything else; and if he was to go into orders, as he had some thoughts, he could get nothing but a curacy, and how was they to live upon

She put in the feather last night

that? – He could not bear to think of her doing no better, and so he begged, if she had the least mind for it, to put an end to the matter directly, and leave him to shift for himself. I heard him say all this as plain as could possibly be. And it was entirely for *her* sake, and upon *her* account, that he said a word about being off, and not upon his own. I will take my oath he never dropped a syllable of being tired of her, or of wishing to marry Miss Morton, or anything like it. But, to be sure, Lucy would not give ear to such kind of talking; so she told him directly (with a great deal about sweet and love, you know, and all that – Oh, la! one can't repeat such kind of things you know) – she told him directly, she had not the least mind in the world to be off, for she could live with him upon a trifle, and how little so ever he might have, she should be very glad to have it all, you know, or something of the kind. So then he was monstrous happy, and talked on some time about what they should do, and they agreed he should take orders directly, and they must wait to be married till he got a living. And just then I could not hear any more, for my cousin called from below to tell me Mrs Richardson was come in her coach, and would take one of us to Kensington Gardens; so I was forced to go into the room and interrupt them, to ask Lucy if she would like to go, but she did not care to leave Edward; so I just run up stairs and put on a pair of silk stockings, and came off with the Richardsons.'

'I do not understand what you mean by interrupting them,' said Elinor; 'you were all in the same room together, were not you?'

'No, indeed, not us. La! Miss Dashwood, do you think people make love when anybody else is by? Oh for shame! To be sure you must know better than that. (Laughing affectedly.) No, no; they were shut up in the drawing-room together, and all I heard was only by listening at the door.'

'How!' cried Elinor; 'have you been repeating to me what you only learnt yourself by listening at the door? I am sorry I did not know it before; for I certainly would not have suffered you to give me particulars of a conversation which you ought not to have known yourself. How could you behave so unfairly by your sister?'

'Oh, la! there is nothing in *that*. I only stood at the door, and heard what I could. And I am sure Lucy would have done just the same by me; for a year or two back, when Martha Sharpe and I had so many secrets together, she never made any bones of hiding in a closet, or behind a chimney-board, on purpose to hear what we said.'

Elinor tried to talk of something else; but Miss Steele could not be kept beyond a couple of minutes, from what was uppermost in her mind.

'Edward talks of going to Oxford soon,' said she, 'but now he is lodging at No.—Pall Mall. What an ill-natured woman his mother is, ain't she? And your brother and sister were not very kind! However, I shan't say anything against them to *you*; and to be sure they did send us home in their own chariot, which was more than I looked for. And for my part, I was all in a fright for fear your sister should ask us for the huswifes she had gave us a day or two before; but however, nothing was said about them, and I took care to keep mine out of sight. Edward have got some business at Oxford, he says; so he must go there for a time; and after *that*, as soon as he can light upon a Bishop, he will be ordained. I wonder what curacy he will get! – Good gracious! (giggling as she spoke) I'd lay my life I know what my cousins will say, when they hear of it. They will tell me I should write to the doctor, to get Edward the curacy of his new living. I know they will; but I am sure I would not do such a thing for all the world – "La!" I shall say directly, "I wonder how you could think of such a thing, *I* write to the doctor, indeed!"'

'Well,' said Elinor, 'it is a comfort to be prepared against the worst. You have got your answer ready.' Miss Steele was going to reply on the same subject, but the approach of her own party made another more necessary.

'Oh, la! here come the Richardsons. I had a vast deal more to say to you, but I must not stay away from them any longer. I assure you they are very genteel people. He makes a monstrous deal of money, and they keep their own coach. I have not time to speak to Mrs Jennings about it myself, but pray tell her I am quite happy to hear she is not in anger against us, and Lady Middleton the same; and if anything should happen to take you and your sister away, and Mrs Jennings should want company, I am sure we should be very glad to come and stay with her for as long a time as she likes. I suppose Lady Middleton won't ask us any more this bout. Goodbye; I am sorry Miss Marianne was not here. Remember me kindly to her. La! if you have not got your spotted muslin on! I wonder you was not afraid of its being torn.'

Such was her parting concern; for after this, she had time only to pay her farewell compliments to Mrs Jennings, before her company was claimed by Mrs Richardson; and Elinor was left in possession of knowledge which might feed her powers of reflection sometime, though she had learnt very little more than what had been already foreseen and foreplanned in her own mind. Edward's marriage with Lucy was as firmly determined on, and the time of its taking place remained as absolutely uncertain, as she had concluded it would be – every thing depended, exactly after her expectation, on his getting that preferment, of which, at present, there seemed not the smallest chance.

As soon as they returned to the carriage, Mrs Jennings was

By listening at the door

eager for information; but as Elinor wished to spread as little as possible intelligence that had in the first place been so unfairly obtained, she confined herself to the brief repetition of such simple particulars, as she felt assured that Lucy, for the sake of her own consequence, would choose to have known.

BELLES AND BALLS

ELIZABETH BENNET, FORCED TO SIT DOWN FOR TWO DANCES DUE TO A SHORTAGE OF MALE PARTNERS AT A BALL HELD IN THE ASSEMBLY ROOM OF THE COUNTRY TOWN OF MERYTON, HEARS A YOUNG ARISTOCRAT, MR FITZWILLIAM DARCY, DECLARE HER TO HIS FRIEND MR BINGLEY A WALLFLOWER NOT HANDSOME ENOUGH TO TEMPT HIM TO ASK HER TO DANCE.

This famous first (non)encounter is uncomfortable and only Elizabeth's lightness of spirit can soften it for herself, her family and her readers. Jane Austen's second novel, developed from an earlier draft called 'First Impressions', was published in January 1813 as *Pride and Prejudice* to acclaim that continues to this day.

That same month, this illustration of a young lady in half full dress appeared in *La Belle Assemblée* and indeed readers of the novel might have felt they recognized Elizabeth in the fashion plate. 'Full dress' refers to the most formal of evening wear worn to a ball or a formal reception while 'Undress' was at the other end of the spectrum: daywear not designed for company. 'Half full dress' falls closer to the formal end and would likely have been appropriate for Meryton's small town ball.

FASHIONS

FOR

FEBRUARY, 1813

EXPLANATION OF THE PRINTS OF FASHION

NO. I – HALF DRESS

Plain frock of amber satin cloth, shot with white and ornamented round the bosom and the waist with a rich white silk trimming, which is called frost work; it is the lightest and most elegant thing we have seen for some time, and is universally worn; a double row of this trimming crosses the breast, and forms the shape of the bosom: the back, which is plain and very broad, is ornamented with pearl buttons, or small silk ones to correspond with the trimming. White lace sleeves, made very full, fastened about the middle of the arm by a broad band of letting in lace, and drawn up by two buttons near the shoulder, while the fullness which falls near the bottom is confined by one; plain demi-train. Regency cap of white lace, with a small front turned up all round, and what was formerly termed a beef-eater's crown; the lace in the crown drawn very full and tightened in by strings of pearl; a tassel of pearls is affixed to the right side of the crown, and a rich amber flower ornaments it in front. Pearl necklace and small cornelian ornament of an oval shape. White kid gloves and slippers.

Half Full Dress

Extract from
PRIDE AND PREJUDICE

Not all that Mrs Bennet, however, with the assistance of her five daughters, could ask on the subject was sufficient to draw from her husband any satisfactory description of Mr Bingley. They attacked him in various ways; with barefaced questions, ingenious suppositions, and distant surmises; but he eluded the skill of them all; and they were at last obliged to accept the second-hand intelligence of their neighbour Lady Lucas. Her report was highly favourable. Sir William had been delighted with him. He was quite young, wonderfully handsome, extremely agreeable, and to crown the whole, he meant to be at the next assembly with a large party. Nothing could be more delightful! To be fond of dancing was a certain step towards falling in love; and very lively hopes of Mr Bingley's heart were entertained.

'If I can but see one of my daughters happily settled at Netherfield,' said Mrs Bennet to her husband, 'and all the others equally well married, I shall have nothing to wish for.'

In a few days Mr Bingley returned Mr Bennet's visit, and sat about ten minutes with him in his library. He had entertained hopes of being admitted to a sight of the young ladies, of whose beauty he had heard much; but he saw only the father. The ladies were somewhat more fortunate, for they had the advantage of ascertaining from an upper window, that he wore a blue coat and rode a black horse.

An invitation to dinner was soon afterwards dispatched; and already had Mrs Bennet planned the courses that were to do credit to her housekeeping, when an answer arrived which deferred it all. Mr Bingley was obliged to be in town the following day, and consequently unable to accept the honour of their invitation, &c. Mrs Bennet was quite disconcerted. She could not imagine what business he could have in town so soon after his arrival in Hertfordshire; and she began to fear that he might be always flying about from one place to another, and never settled at Netherfield as he ought to be. Lady Lucas quieted her fears a little by starting the idea of his being gone to London only to get a large party for the ball; and a report soon followed that Mr Bingley was to bring twelve ladies and seven gentlemen with him to the assembly. The girls grieved over such a number of ladies; but were comforted the day before the ball by hearing, that instead of twelve, he had brought only six with him from London, his five sisters and a cousin. And when the party entered the assembly room, it consisted of only five altogether; Mr Bingley, his two sisters, the husband of the eldest, and another young man.

Mr Bingley was good looking and gentlemanlike; he had a pleasant countenance, and easy, unaffected manners. His sisters were fine women, with an air of decided fashion. His brother-in-law, Mr Hurst, merely looked the gentleman; but his friend Mr Darcy soon drew the attention of the room by his fine, tall person, handsome features, noble mien; and the report which was in general circulation within five minutes after his entrance, of his having ten thousand a year. The gentlemen pronounced him to be a fine figure of a man, the ladies declared he was much handsomer than Mr Bingley, and he was looked at with great admiration for about half the evening, till his manners gave a disgust which turned the tide of his popularity; for he was

When the party entered

discovered to be proud, to be above his company, and above being pleased; and not all his large estate in Derbyshire could then save him from having a most forbidding, disagreeable countenance, and being unworthy to be compared with his friend.

Mr Bingley had soon made himself acquainted with all the principal people in the room; he was lively and unreserved, danced every dance, was angry that the ball closed so early, and talked of giving one himself at Netherfield. Such amiable qualities must speak for themselves. What a contrast between him and his friend! Mr Darcy danced only once with Mrs Hurst and once with Miss Bingley, declined being introduced to any other lady, and spent the rest of the evening in walking about the room, speaking occasionally to one of his own party. His character was decided. He was the proudest, most disagreeable man in the world, and everybody hoped that he would never come there again. Amongst the most violent against him was Mrs Bennet, whose dislike of his general behaviour, was sharpened into particular resentment, by his having slighted one of her daughters.

Elizabeth Bennet had been obliged, by the scarcity of gentlemen, to sit down for two dances; and during part of that time, Mr Darcy had been standing near enough for her to overhear a conversation between him and Mr Bingley, who came from the dance for a few minutes, to press his friend to join it.

'Come, Darcy,' said he, 'I must have you dance. I hate to see you standing about by yourself in this stupid manner. You had much better dance.'

'I certainly shall not. You know how I detest it, unless I am particularly acquainted with my partner. At such an assembly as this, it would be insupportable. Your sisters are engaged, and there is not another woman in the room, whom it would not be a punishment to me to stand up with.'

'I would not be so fastidious as you are,' cried Bingley, 'for a kingdom! Upon my honour, I never met with so many pleasant girls in my life, as I have this evening; and there are several of them you see uncommonly pretty.'

'*You* are dancing with the only handsome girl in the room,' said Mr Darcy, looking at the eldest Miss Bennet.

'Oh! she is the most beautiful creature I ever beheld! But there is one of her sisters sitting down just behind you, who is very pretty, and I dare say, very agreeable. Do let me ask my partner to introduce you.'

'Which do you mean?' and turning round, he looked for a moment at Elizabeth, till catching her eye, he withdrew his own and coldly said, 'She is tolerable; but not handsome enough to tempt *me*; and I am in no humour at present to give consequence to young ladies who are slighted by other men. You had better return to your partner and enjoy her smiles, for you are wasting your time with me.'

Mr Bingley followed his advice. Mr Darcy walked off; and Elizabeth remained with no very cordial feelings towards him. She told the story however with great spirit among her friends; for she had a lively, playful disposition, which delighted in anything ridiculous.

PETTICOATS, PRIDE AND PREJUDICE

Muddy autumnal paths do not impede Elizabeth Bennet from walking three miles to tend to her sister Jane, who has fallen ill as the result of riding in driving rain to visit her new friends, the Bingley sisters.

The Austen sisters regularly walked the three-mile round trip from their home in Chawton to the main town of Alton. And 'walking dress' needed to be stout: an outer garment (a cloak likely of wool), a hat or bonnet and probably half boots that lace up to the ankle.

In the more fashionable metropolitan world, 'walking dress' might also be called 'promenade dress' and the latter, though worn outdoors, was more for display than transport. But this 'Autumnal Walking Dress' captures its potential attractions, including the brilliancy of complexion Darcy admires and the muddy petticoats that might draw the eye to the more-than-usual display of ankle.

La Belle Assemblée was engaged in early product placement by promoting the shapelines of the corset worn beneath the dress and tight-fitting jacket. The corset happened to be designed and marketed by Mary Ann Bell, daughter-in-law to the magazine's owner, John Bell.

FASHIONS

FOR

OCTOBER, 1814

EXPLANATION OF THE PRINTS OF FASHION
AUTUMNAL WALKING DRESS

Jaconet muslin high dress, with a triple flounce of muslin embroidery round the edge, and slightly scalloped; a row of worked points surmounts the top flounce. The body is composed of jaconet muslin and letting-in lace; the former cut in broad strips and sewed full to the latter, which is about an inch in breadth; this body is made up to the throat, but has no collar: the shape is the same as last month except that the back is a little broader. Long sleeve of muslin and lace to correspond with the body. Spenceret of rose-coloured velvet of a form the most elegantly simple and tasteful that we have seen; it is very short in the waist, and tight to the shape; it is ornamented at top by a lace frill, and is cut so as to cover the bosom but to leave the neck bare. This spenceret is very much admired, and it is certainly truly elegant, but it owes its principal attraction to the corset over which it is worn, and certainly nothing was ever so well calculated to display a fine shape to advantage as the Circassian corset, which has been patronized and recommended with incredible celerity by ladies of the highest distinction, who are unanimous in declaring it to be the only corset ever introduced that has in every way answered the encomiums bestowed upon it. The superior ease, gracefulness, and elegance which it gives to the female figure, are too obvious to need a comment; while on the other hand, its beneficial effects upon the health are daily attested by ladies who rejoice in the success of an invention which has freed them from the tortures inflicted by whalebone, steel, &c. We must not omit to observe that the walking bonnet of this month, which is composed of white satin and rose-coloured velvet, and ornamented with a plume of white feathers, will certainly become general, as it is a most elegant bonnet; it is worn over a small white lace cap. Rose-coloured jane, or leather, boots, and Limerick gloves.

The above dress was invented by Mrs. Bell, Inventress of the ladies' *Chapeau Bras*, at her *Magazin des Modes.* No. 26 Charlotte-street, Bedford-square.

Morning Walking Dress

Extract from
PRIDE AND PREJUDICE

Breakfast was scarcely over when a servant from Netherfield brought the following note for Elizabeth:

> My Dearest Lizzy – I find myself very unwell this morning, which, I suppose, is to be imputed to my getting wet through yesterday. My kind friends will not hear of my returning home till I am better. They insist also on my seeing Mr Jones – therefore do not be alarmed if you should hear of his having been to me – and excepting a sore throat and headache there is not much the matter with me.
>
> 'Yours, &c.'

'Well, my dear,' said Mr Bennet, when Elizabeth had read the note aloud, 'if your daughter should have a dangerous fit of illness, if she should die, it would be a comfort to know that it was all in pursuit of Mr Bingley, and under your orders.'

'Oh! I am not at all afraid of her dying. People do not die of little trifling colds. She will be taken good care of. As long as she stays there, it is all very well. I would go and see her, if I could have the carriage.'

Elizabeth, feeling really anxious, was determined to go to her, though the carriage was not to be had; and as she was no horsewoman, walking was her only alternative. She declared her resolution.

'How can you be so silly,' cried her mother, 'as to think of such a thing, in all this dirt! You will not be fit to be seen when you get there.'

'I shall be very fit to see Jane – which is all I want.'

'Is this a hint to me, Lizzy,' said her father, 'to send for the horses?'

'No, indeed. I do not wish to avoid the walk. The distance is nothing, when one has a motive; only three miles. I shall be back by dinner.'

'I admire the activity of your benevolence,' observed Mary, 'but every impulse of feeling should be guided by reason; and, in my opinion, exertion should always be in proportion to what is required.'

'We will go as far as Meryton with you,' said Catherine and Lydia. Elizabeth accepted their company, and the three young ladies set off together.

'If we make haste,' said Lydia, as they walked along, 'perhaps we may see something of Captain Carter before he goes.'

In Meryton they parted; the two youngest repaired to the lodgings of one of the officers' wives, and Elizabeth continued her walk alone, crossing field after field at a quick pace, jumping over stiles and springing over puddles with impatient activity, and finding herself at last within view of the house, with weary ankles, dirty stockings, and a face glowing with the warmth of exercise.

She was shown into the breakfast parlour, where all but Jane were assembled, and where her appearance created a great deal of surprise. That she should have walked three miles so early in the day, in such dirty weather, and by herself, was almost incredible to Mrs Hurst and Miss Bingley; and Elizabeth was convinced that they held her in contempt for it. She was received, however, very politely by them; and in their brother's manners there was something better than politeness; there was good humour and kindness. Mr Darcy said very little, and Mr Hurst nothing at all. The former was divided between admiration of the brilliancy which exercise had given to her complexion, and doubt as to the occasion's justifying her coming so far alone. The latter was thinking only of his breakfast.

Her enquiries after her sister were not very favourably answered. Miss Bennet had slept ill, and though up, was very feverish and not well enough to leave her room. Elizabeth was glad to be taken to her immediately; and Jane, who had only been withheld by the fear of giving alarm or inconvenience, from expressing in her note how much she longed for such a visit, was delighted at her entrance. She was not equal, however, to much conversation, and when Miss Bingley left them together, could attempt little beside expressions of gratitude for the extraordinary kindness she was treated with. Elizabeth silently attended her.

When breakfast was over, they were joined by the sisters; and Elizabeth began to like them herself, when she saw how much affection and solicitude they showed for Jane. The apothecary came, and having examined his patient, said, as might be supposed, that she had caught a violent cold, and that they must endeavour to get the better of it; advised her to return to bed, and promised her some draughts. The advice was followed readily, for the feverish symptoms increased, and her head ached acutely. Elizabeth did not quit her room for a moment, nor were the other ladies often absent; the gentlemen being out, they had in fact nothing to do elsewhere.

When the clock struck three, Elizabeth felt that she must go; and very unwillingly said so. Miss Bingley offered her the carriage, and she only wanted a little pressing to accept it, when Jane testified such concern in parting with her, that Miss Bingley was obliged to convert the offer of the chaise into an invitation to remain at Netherfield for the present. Elizabeth most thankfully consented, and a servant was dispatched to Longbourn to acquaint the family with her stay, and bring back a supply of clothes.

WALKING TO MERYTON

THREE YOUNG WOMEN IN WHITE GOWNS AND FLUTTERING RIBBONS CLUSTER TOGETHER ON A STREET CORNER; THE GLANCES OF TWO OF THEM ARE CAUGHT BY SOMETHING, PERHAPS A SMART OFFICER, OR A NEW MUSLIN, ITEMS SO ALLURING TO KITTY AND LYDIA, THE YOUNGER BENNET SISTERS OF *PRIDE AND PREJUDICE*.

Jane and Elizabeth walk into Meryton with their chattering younger sisters and their tiresome cousin, the curate Mr Collins. The party stop to talk to the charming officer Mr Wickham and when Mr Darcy and Mr Bingley join them on horseback, Elizabeth observes the mutual discomfort of Darcy and Wickham.

Embellishing headwear was one way that women could make their walking dress stand out. In a letter from 27 October 1798, Austen speaks of her 'operations on my hat'. The hats in the illustration are especially flamboyant and fluttering, as are Kitty and Lydia in *Pride and Prejudice*. Two of the girls are wearing straw hats with wide brims, allowing them to both look and conceal their looks, whereas the simple turban bonnet of the third woman leaves her face more exposed but also gives her a better and more comprehensive view, an advantage Elizabeth Bennet has over her sisters.

FASHIONS

FOR

JUNE, 1808

EXPLANATION OF THE PRINTS OF FASHION

ENGLISH COSTUME

NO. 1

A plain cambric or jaconet muslin dress, made a walking length; scalloped at the feet and wrist with high gored bosom, and long sleeve of net. A spencer of silver lilac sarsnet, with bosom and cuffs, ornamented *à-la-Militaire*. Simple turban bonnet, composed of the same material as the spencer. The hair in alternate bands and ringlets. Gloves and shoes of lemon-coloured kid; and parasol of shaded green sarsnet. It is as well to observe that with this kind of bonnet is usually worn a short veil of white lace, suspended from the edge next the hair.

NO. 2

A light dress of blossom-coloured muslin, over white cambric, with waistcoat bosom, and deep scalloped collar and cuffs. A large gipsy hat of straw, or imperial chip, tied across the crown with a silk handkerchief, of the same shade, or one of white brocade sarsnet. A veil of Mecklin lace, thrown negligently over the front of the hat, so as agreeably to shade the countenance. Small

French watch, worn on the outside. Shoes of purple kid, or live jean. Gloves of York-tan. Brown, green, or purple parasol, with a deep fringed awning.

NO. 3

A simple frock of French cambric, buttoned up the back, with round bosom, and plain sleeve, with frock cuff. A Spanish vest of pale blue, or French grey sarsnet, with short French sleeve, lapelled bosom, and pointed skirt, finished with correspondent tassels. A pale amber, or lemon-coloured scarf, of Chinese silk, twisted negligently round the throat, the ends flowing in varied drapery or restrained by the graceful disposition of the hand. A cottage poke-bonnet of fine straw, simply ornamented with a bow of white ribband on the right side. Gold filigree earrings of the hoop form. Hair in irregular curls, partially confined with a band. Gloves of Limerick, and shoes of grey kid.

Fashionable Spring Walking Dresses

Extract from

PRIDE AND PREJUDICE

Lydia's intention of walking to Meryton was not forgotten; every sister except Mary agreed to go with her; and Mr Collins was to attend them, at the request of Mr Bennet, who was most anxious to get rid of him, and have his library to himself; for thither Mr Collins had followed him after breakfast, and there he would continue, nominally engaged with one of the largest folios in the collection, but really talking to Mr Bennet, with little cessation, of his house and garden at Hunsford. Such doings discomposed Mr Bennet exceedingly. In his library he had been always sure of leisure and tranquillity; and though prepared, as he told Elizabeth, to meet with folly and conceit in every other room in the house, he was used to be free from them there; his civility, therefore, was most prompt in inviting Mr Collins to join his daughters in their walk; and Mr Collins, being in fact much better fitted for a walker than a reader, was extremely well pleased to close his large book, and go.

In pompous nothings on his side, and civil assents on that of his cousins, their time passed till they entered Meryton. The attention of the younger ones was then no longer to be gained by *him*. Their eyes were immediately wandering up in the street in quest of the officers, and nothing less than a very smart bonnet indeed, or a really new muslin in a shop window, could recall them.

But the attention of every lady was soon caught by a young man, whom they had never seen before, of most gentleman-like appearance, walking with an officer on the other side of the way. The officer was the very Mr Denny, concerning whose return from London Lydia came to enquire, and he bowed as they passed. All were struck with the stranger's air, all wondered who he could be, and Kitty and Lydia, determined if possible to find out, led the way across the street, under pretence of wanting something in an opposite shop, and fortunately had just gained the pavement when the two gentlemen turning back had reached the same spot. Mr Denny addressed them directly, and entreated permission to introduce his friend, Mr Wickham, who had returned with him the day before from town, and he was happy to say had accepted a commission in their corps. This was exactly as it should be; for the young man wanted only regimentals to make him completely charming. His appearance was greatly in his favour; he had all the best part of beauty, a fine countenance, a good figure, and very pleasing address. The introduction was followed up on his side by a happy readiness of conversation – a readiness at the same time perfectly correct and unassuming; and the whole party were still standing and talking together very agreeably, when the sound of horses drew their notice, and Darcy and Bingley were seen riding down the street. On distinguishing the ladies of the group, the two gentlemen came directly towards them, and began the usual civilities. Bingley was the principal spokesman, and Miss Bennet the principal object. He was then, he said, on his way to Longbourn on purpose to enquire after her. Mr Darcy corroborated it with a bow, and was beginning to determine not to fix his eyes on Elizabeth, when they were suddenly arrested by the sight of the stranger, and Elizabeth happening to see the countenance of both as they looked at each other, was all astonishment at the effect of the meeting. Both changed colour, one looked white, the other red. Mr Wickham, after a few moments, touched his hat – a salutation which Mr Darcy just deigned to return. What could be the meaning of it? – It was impossible to imagine; it was impossible not to long to know.

In another minute Mr Bingley, but without seeming to have noticed what passed, took leave and rode on with his friend.

Mr Denny and Mr Wickham walked with the young ladies to the door of Mr Philips's house, and then made their bows, in spite of Miss Lydia's pressing entreaties that they would come in, and even in spite of Mrs Philips throwing up the parlour window, and loudly seconding the invitation.

Mrs Philips was always glad to see her nieces, and the two eldest, from their recent absence, were particularly welcome, and she was eagerly expressing her surprise at their sudden return home, which, as their own carriage had not fetched them, she should have known nothing about, if she had not happened to see Mr Jones's shop boy in the street, who had told her that they were not to send any more draughts to Netherfield because the Miss Bennets were come away, when her civility was claimed towards Mr Collins by Jane's introduction of him. She received him with her very best politeness, which he returned with as much more, apologising for his intrusion, without any previous acquaintance with her, which he could not help flattering himself however might be justified by his relationship to the young ladies who introduced him to her notice. Mrs Philips was quite awed by such an excess of good breeding; but her contemplation of one stranger was soon put an end to by exclamations and enquiries about the other, of whom, however, she could only tell her nieces what they already knew, that Mr Denny had brought him from London, and that he was to have a lieutenant's commission in the —shire. She had been watching him the last hour, she said, as he walked up and down the street, and had Mr Wickham appeared Kitty and Lydia would certainly have continued the occupation, but unluckily no one passed the windows now except a few of the officers, who in comparison with the stranger, were become 'stupid, disagreeable fellows'. Some of them were to dine with the Philipses the next day, and their aunt promised to make her husband call on Mr Wickham, and give him an invitation also, if the family from Longbourn would come in the evening. This was agreed to, and Mrs Philips protested that they would have a nice comfortable noisy game of lottery tickets, and a little bit of hot supper afterwards. The prospect of such delights was very cheering, and they parted in mutual good spirits. Mr Collins repeated his apologies in quitting the room, and was assured with unwearying civility that they were perfectly needless.

As they walked home, Elizabeth related to Jane what she had seen pass between the two gentlemen; but though Jane would have defended either or both, had they appeared to be wrong, she could no more explain such behaviour than her sister.

Mr Collins on his return highly gratified Mrs Bennet by admiring Mrs Philips's manners and politeness. He protested that except Lady Catherine and her daughter, he had never seen a more elegant woman; for she had not only received him with the utmost civility, but had even pointedly included him in her invitation for the next evening, although utterly unknown to her before. Something he supposed might be attributed to his connection with them, but yet he had never met with so much attention in the whole course of his life.

CRAPE EXPECTATIONS

By November 1813, now a month short of thirty-eight years of age, Jane Austen was obliged to 'leave off being young', as she says in the following letter she composed to her older sister Cassandra when she was visiting their brother Edward Knight and his family at his estate at Godmersham Park near Canterbury in Kent.

Nonetheless, she was still very busy attending a concert, catching up with friends and family, making new friends, and – especially – planning her dress for an upcoming ball, a 'China crape'. This was not the 'crape' reserved for mourning but rather a silk woven in India or China. Both Jane and Cassandra were proud possessors of dresses in this lightweight textile, possibly brought back to them by their sailor brother Francis from a trip from Canton to England via Madras in 1810.

The fashions for June 1813, earlier that year, included a 'Frock of straw-colour crape'. And the 'General Observations' noted that: 'For full dress, crape is universal; the frock which we have given in our Plate is the first in estimation'. Jane Austen reported in a letter of 5 March 1814 that she had decided to trim a lilac sarsnet dress with the same black satin ribbon that features on her 'China crape'. Mature elegance is the effect sought both in the fashion plate and Jane Austen's imagination.

FASHIONS

FOR

JUNE, 1813

EXPLANATION OF THE PRINTS OF FASHION

NO. 2 – BALL DRESS

Frock of straw-colour crape, over a white sarsnet petticoat; it is made a walking length, open behind and trimmed round with white silk fancy twist. A rich French lace set on full, edges it at bottom, and it fastens up behind with bows of white ribband. The body of this dress is formed in a novel and peculiarly becoming style, it is made very low all round the bosom and back of the neck. The back, as our fair readers will see by the Plate, is shaped by the trimming which goes up on each side; it is very narrow at bottom, and displays the shape to great advantage; the front is composed of lace set in to form the shape of the bosom. Sleeves about half way to the elbow of crape and white lace let in. Hair turned up behind *à-la-Grecque*, and braided on one side of the forehead; on the other a few careless ringlets fall over, and nearly shade the eye-brow; a light laurel wreath is put much to one side. Necklaces, ear-rings, and bracelets of pearl. White kid gloves, and white figured silk slippers cut very low in front. An azure silk scarf which is very light, but extremely rich and beautiful, is thrown occasionally over the shoulders by some of our *elegantés*.

Evening Dress

Extract from
LETTERS OF JANE AUSTEN

LXX
Godmersham Park: Saturday (Nov 6), 1813

MY DEAREST CASSANDRA,
Having half-an-hour before breakfast (very snug, in my own room, lovely morning, excellent fire – fancy me!) I will give you some account of the last two days. And yet, what is there to be told? I shall get foolishly minute unless I cut the matter short.

We met only the Bretons at Chilham Castle, besides a Mr. and Mrs. Osborne and a Miss Lee staying in the house, and were only fourteen altogether. My brother and Fanny thought it the pleasantest party they had ever known there, and I was very well entertained by bits and scraps. I had long wanted to see Dr. Breton, and his wife amuses me very much with her affected refinement and elegance. Miss Lee I found very conversable; she admires Crabbe as she ought. She is at an age of reason, ten years older than myself at least. She was at the famous ball of Chilham Castle, so of course you remember her.

By-the-bye, as I must leave off being young, I find many *douceurs* in being a sort of *chaperon*, for I am put on the sofa near the fire, and can drink as much wine as I like. We had music in the evening: Fanny and Miss Wildman played, and Mr. James Wildman sat close by and listened, or pretended to listen.

Yesterday was a day of dissipation all through: first came Sir Brook to dissipate us before breakfast; then there was a call from Mr. Sherer, then a regular morning visit from Lady Honeywood in her way home from Eastwell; then Sir Brook and Edward set off; then we dined (five in number) at half-past four; then we had coffee; and at six Miss Clewes, Fanny, and I drove away. We had a beautiful night for our frisks. We were earlier than we need have been, but after a time Lady B. and her two companions appeared – we had kept places for them; and there we sat, all six in a row, under a side wall, I between Lucy Foote and Miss Clewes.

Lady B. was much what I expected; I could not determine whether she was rather handsome or very plain. I liked her for being in a hurry to have the concert over and get away, and for getting away at last with a great deal of decision and promptness, not waiting to compliment and dawdle and fuss about seeing *dear Fanny*, who was half the evening in another part of the room with her friends the Plumptres. I am growing too minute, so I will go to breakfast.

When the concert was over, Mrs. Harrison and I found each other out, and had a very comfortable little complimentary friendly chat. She is a sweet woman – still quite a sweet woman in herself, and so like her sister! I could almost have thought I was speaking to Mr. Lefroy. She introduced me to her daughter, whom I think pretty, but most dutifully inferior to *la Mère Beauté*. The Faggs and the Hammonds were there – Wm. Hammond the only young man of renown. *Miss* looked very handsome, but I prefer her little smiling flirting sister Julia.

I was just introduced at last to Mary Plumptre, but should hardly know her again. She was delighted with *me*, however, good enthusiastic soul! And Lady B. found me handsomer than she expected, so you see I am not so very bad as you might think for.

It was 12 before we reached home. We were all dog-tired, but pretty well to-day: Miss Clewes says she has not caught cold, and Fanny's does not seem worse. I was so tired that I began to wonder how I should get through the ball next Thursday; but there will be so much variety then in walking about, and probably so much less heat, than perhaps I may not feel it more. My China crape is still kept for the ball. Enough of the concert.

HEALTH AND HORSEBACK

In *Mansfield Park*, Fanny Price, a poor relative taken as a child into the wealthy household of Sir Thomas Bertram, is physically frail but morally strong. When their old grey pony dies, her affectionate cousin, Edmund, insists she needs a horse for her regular health-giving rides, so he exchanges his third horse for a suitable mare.

His mother, Lady Bertram, is too lazy to think of it and their aunt, self-important Mrs Norris, thoroughly disapproves of any attention being given to obscure Fanny.

La Belle Assemblée provided many examples of riding dress but rarely depicted women on horseback. This, from Spring 1807, is an unusual example described as the height of Parisian fashion. Equestrian dress for women was introduced in the seventeenth century in the shape of the riding habit. The overall impression was expected to be masculine, with a long coat that buttoned from bosom to hem and a military-style tall hat. In order to ride side-saddle but keep the legs covered, the habit had a long train that could be held up by a tie on the inside of the skirt when walking. This outfit would certainly be too flashy for modest Fanny, though her rival, Mary Crawford, would surely have sought to cut this kind of dash.

FASHIONS
FOR
APRIL, 1807

EXPLANATION OF THE PRINTS OF FASHION

PARISIAN COSTUME

NO. 3

Represents a Parisian lady, mounted in the most fashionable style, for the *Long Champs* and *Elysées*, at Paris.—An equestrian habit of fine seal-wool cloth, with elastic strap; the colour blue (but olive, or puce, are equally esteemed), with convex buttons of dead gold. The habit to sit high in the neck behind, lapelled in front, and buttoned twice at the small of the waist; a high plaited frill of cambric, uniting at the bosom where the habit closes. A jockey bonnet of the same materials as composes the habit, finished with a band and tuft in front. Hair in dishevelled crop. York tan gloves; and demi-boots of purple kid, laced with jonquille chord.

A French Lady on Horseback

Extract from
MANSFIELD PARK

Lady Bertram did not go into public with her daughters. She was too indolent even to accept a mother's gratification in witnessing their success and enjoyment at the expense of any personal trouble, and the charge was made over to her sister, who desired nothing better than a post of such honourable representation, and very thoroughly relished the means it afforded her of mixing in society without having horses to hire.

Fanny had no share in the festivities of the season; but she enjoyed being avowedly useful as her aunt's companion, when they called away the rest of the family; and as Miss Lee had left Mansfield, she naturally became everything to Lady Bertram during the night of a ball or a party. She talked to her, listened to her, read to her; and the tranquillity of such evenings, her perfect security in such a tête-á-tête from any sound of unkindness, was unspeakably welcome to a mind which had seldom known a pause in its alarms or embarrassments. As to her cousins' gaieties, she loved to hear an account of them, especially of the balls, and whom Edmund had danced with; but thought too lowly of her own situation to imagine she should ever be admitted to the same, and listened therefore without an idea of any nearer concern in them. Upon the whole, it was a comfortable winter to her; for though it brought no William to England, the never failing hope of his arrival was worth much.

The ensuing spring deprived her of her valued friend the old grey pony, and for some time she was in danger of feeling the loss in her health as well as in her affections, for in spite of the acknowledged importance of her riding on horseback, no measures were taken for mounting her again, 'because,' as it was observed by her aunts, 'she might ride one of her cousins' horses at any time when they did not want them;' and as the Miss Bertrams regularly wanted their horses every fine day, and had no idea of carrying their obliging manners to the sacrifice of any real pleasure, that time of course never came. They took their cheerful rides in the fine mornings of April and May; and Fanny either sat at home the whole day with one aunt, or walked beyond her strength at the instigation of the other; Lady Bertram holding exercise to be as unnecessary for everybody as it was unpleasant to herself; and Mrs Norris, who was walking all day, thinking everybody ought to walk as much. Edmund was absent at this time, or the evil would have been earlier remedied. When he returned to understand how Fanny was situated, and perceive its ill effects, there seemed with him but one thing to be done, and that 'Fanny must have a horse,' was the resolute declaration with which he opposed whatever could be urged by the supineness of his mother, or the economy of his aunt, to make it appear unimportant. Mrs Norris could not help thinking that some steady old thing might be found among the numbers belonging to the Park, that would do vastly well, or that one might be borrowed of the steward, or that perhaps Dr Grant might now and then lend them the pony he sent to the post. She could not but consider it as absolutely unnecessary, and even improper, that Fanny should have a regular lady's horse of her own in the style of her cousins. She was sure Sir Thomas had never intended it; and she must say, that to be making such a purchase in his absence, and adding to the great expenses of his stable at a time when a large part of his income was unsettled, seemed to her very unjustifiable. 'Fanny must have a horse,' was Edmund's only reply. Mrs Norris could not see it in the same light. Lady Bertram did; she entirely agreed with her son as to the necessity of it, and as to its being considered necessary by his father – she only pleaded against there being any hurry, she only wanted him to wait till Sir Thomas's return, and then Sir Thomas might settle it all himself. He would be at home in September, and where would be the harm of only waiting till September?

Though Edmund was much more displeased with his aunt than with his mother, as evincing least regard for her niece, he could not help paying more attention to what she said, and at length determined on a method of proceeding which would obviate the risk of his father's thinking he had done too much, and at the same time procure for Fanny the immediate means of exercise, which he could not bear she should be without. He had three horses of his own, but not one that would carry a woman. Two of them were hunters; the third, a useful road-horse: this third he resolved to exchange for one that his cousin might ride; he knew where such a one was to be met with, and having once made up his mind, the whole business was soon completed. The new mare proved a treasure; with a very little trouble, she became exactly calculated for the purpose, and Fanny was then put in almost full possession of her. She had not supposed before, that anything could ever suit her like the old grey pony; but her delight in Edmund's mare was far beyond any former pleasure of the sort; and the addition it was ever receiving in the consideration of that kindness from which her pleasure sprung, was beyond all her words to express. She regarded her cousin as an example of everything good and great, as possessing worth, which no one but herself could ever appreciate, and as entitled to such gratitude from her, as no feelings could be strong enough to pay. Her sentiments towards him were compounded of all that was respectful, grateful, confiding, and tender.

PLAYING THE PART

In this scene from *Mansfield Park*, Fanny and Edmund are assessing the character of Mary Crawford, who is staying with Fanny's brother, Henry. Edmund is increasingly bewitched but Fanny reminds him of the inappropriate remarks made by Mary about her own uncle. The sight of Mary Crawford playing her harp by an open window is enough for Edmund to put aside these doubts.

The Austens were a musical family and Jane was accomplished on the pianoforte. The harp, however, was associated with more flashy performances. Staying in London with her brother Henry in 1815, Jane writes to Cassandra about enjoying at a party 'From 7 to 8 the harp'. This was the instrument of captivating Eliza, cousin to the Austen siblings and Henry's first wife, who was the inspiration for flirtatious Mary Crawford.

La Belle Assemblée illustrates here a performer's concert dress in this lovely image of a player with her harp. The player's dress is Polonaise, a fancy name for an open robe that was not hitched up. It was often worn in public places but also by people of fashion as 'undress' at home. Bodices were fastened at the bosom and continued into the overskirt, giving a flaring shape that echoes the curve of the harp itself. So too the scene of Mary playing is in harmony 'with a harp as elegant as herself'.

FASHIONS

FOR

DECEMBER, 1809

EXPLANATION OF THE PRINTS OF FASHION

ENGLISH COSTUME

NO. I – CONCERT-ROOM FULL DRESS

A Polanese dress of green and yellow double twilled sarsnet; worn over a drapery of rich white lace, with long sleeves; confined at the bosom, the waist, and on the arms by topaz brooches; ornamented with silver trimming and tassels; a body and train of yellow satin. A Grecian head-dress, composed of silver spangled crape and white satin, marked off at the crown by a wreath of green foil, and finished on the left side with a silver cord and tassels, worn with two white ostrich feathers tipped with green. Topaz necklace and earrings. Shoes and gloves of pale yellow, white, or green. The hair in full short ringlet curls.

Concert Room Full Dress

Extract from

MANSFIELD PARK

'Well Fanny, and how do you like Miss Crawford *now*?' said Edmund the next day, after thinking some time on the subject himself. 'How did you like her yesterday?'

'Very well – very much. I like to hear her talk. She entertains me; and she is so extremely pretty, that I have great pleasure in looking at her.'

'It is her countenance that is so attractive. She has a wonderful play of feature! But was there nothing in her conversation that struck you, Fanny, as not quite right?'

'Oh! yes, she ought not to have spoken of her uncle as she did. I was quite astonished. An uncle with whom she has been living so many years, and who, whatever his faults may be, is so very fond of her brother, treating him, they say, quite like a son. I could not have believed it!'

'I thought you would be struck. It was very wrong – very indecorous.'

'And very ungrateful I think.'

'Ungrateful is a strong word. I do not know that her uncle has any claim to her *gratitude*; his wife certainly had; and it is the warmth of her respect for her aunt's memory which misleads her here. She is awkwardly circumstanced. With such warm feelings and lively spirits it must be difficult to do justice to her affection for Mrs Crawford, without throwing a shade on the admiral. I do not pretend to know which was most to blame in their disagreements, though the admiral's present conduct might incline one to the side of his wife: but it is natural and amiable that Miss Crawford should acquit her aunt entirely. I do not censure her *opinions*; but there certainly is impropriety in making them public.'

'Do not you think,' said Fanny, after a little consideration, 'that this impropriety is a reflection itself upon Mrs Crawford, as her niece has been entirely brought up by her? She cannot have given her right notions of what was due to the admiral.'

'That is a fair remark. Yes, we must suppose the faults of the niece to have been those of the aunt; and it makes one more sensible of the disadvantages she has been under. But I think her present home must do her good. Mrs Grant's manners are just what they ought to be. She speaks of her brother with a very pleasing affection.'

'Yes, except as to his writing her such short letters. She made me almost laugh; but I cannot rate so very highly the love or good nature of a brother, who will not give himself the trouble of writing anything worth reading, to his sisters, when they are separated. I am sure William would never have used *me* so, under any circumstances. And what right had she to suppose, that *you* would not write long letters when you were absent?'

'The right of a lively mind, Fanny, seizing whatever may contribute to its own amusement or that of others; perfectly allowable, when untinctured by ill humour or roughness; and there is not a shadow of either in the countenance or manner of Miss Crawford, nothing sharp, or loud, or coarse. She is perfectly feminine, except in the instances we have been speaking of. *There* she cannot be justified. I am glad you saw it all as I did.'

Having formed her mind and gained her affections, he had

a good chance of her thinking like him; though at this period, and on this subject, there began now to be some danger of dissimilarity, for he was in a line of admiration of Miss Crawford, which might lead him where Fanny could not follow. Miss Crawford's attractions did not lessen. The harp arrived, and rather added to her beauty, wit, and good humour, for she played with the greatest obligingness, with an expression and taste which were peculiarly becoming, and there was something clever to be said at the close of every air. Edmund was at the parsonage every day to be indulged with his favourite instrument; one morning secured an invitation for the next, for the lady could not be unwilling to have a listener, and everything was soon in a fair train.

A young woman, pretty, lively, with a harp as elegant as herself; and both placed near a window, cut down to the ground, and opening on a little lawn, surrounded by shrubs in the rich foliage of summer, was enough to catch any man's heart. The season, the scene, the air, were all favourable to tenderness and sentiment. Mrs Grant and her tambour frame were not without their use; it was all in harmony; and as everything will turn to account when love is once set going, even the sandwich tray, and Dr Grant doing the honours of it, were worth looking at. Without studying the business, however, or knowing what he was about, Edmund was beginning at the end of a week of such intercourse, to be a good deal in love; and to the credit of the lady it may be added, that without his being a man of the world or an elder brother, without any of the arts of flattery or the gaieties of small talk, he began to be agreeable to her. She felt it to be so, though she had not foreseen and could hardly understand it; for he was not pleasant by any common rule, he talked no nonsense, he paid no compliments, his opinions were unbending, his attentions tranquil and simple. There was a charm, perhaps, in his sincerity, his steadiness, his integrity, which Miss Crawford might be equal to feel, though not equal to discuss with herself. She did not think very much about it, however; he pleased her for the present; she liked to have him near her; it was enough.

Fanny could not wonder that Edmund was at the parsonage every morning; she would gladly have been there too, might she have gone in uninvited and unnoticed to hear the harp; neither could she wonder, that when the evening stroll was over, and the two families parted again, he should think it right to attend Mrs Grant and her sister to their home, while Mr Crawford was devoted to the ladies of the park; but she thought it a very bad exchange, and if Edmund were not there to mix the wine and water for her, would rather go without it than not. She was a little surprised that he could spend so many hours with Miss Crawford, and not see more of the sort of fault which he had already observed, and of which *she* was almost always reminded by a something of the same nature whenever she was in her company; but so it was. Edmund was fond of speaking to her of Miss Crawford, but he seemed to think it enough that the admiral had since been spared; and she scrupled to point out her own remarks to him, lest it should appear like ill-nature.

PUGS AND PELISSES

The only garment that survives of Jane Austen's is a brown silk pelisse she acquired some time between 1812 and August 1814 when it is mentioned in a letter to her sister. It probably dates from the period in which *Mansfield Park* was composed (1811–1813).

A pelisse is a straight coat closed in front with a tie. Jane's pelisse was, like the one illustrated in *La Belle Assemblée*, an autumnal piece. It was patterned with falling oak leaves in gold and adorned with silk cord, whereas the pelisse in our illustration is decorated with acorn tassels and ornamented with silver frogs.

Jane rarely describes what her characters are wearing but she does provide them with accessories that communicate personality. In the case of lazy, affectionate Lady Bertram she is always accompanied by her dog, in her case a pug. Pugs were bred in China to adorn the laps of Chinese sovereigns during the Shang dynasty c. 400BC. They are, then, like Lady Bertram, creatures of indolence. In this scene, we see Lady Bertram assume that Fanny will accept the proposal of Henry Crawford. In offering her a pug from Pug's next litter she also imagines Fanny as another version of her lapdog – an accessory to her wealth and power – and a prospective future version of herself, raised up to privilege through marriage.

FASHIONS

FOR

OCTOBER, 1810

EXPLANATION OF THE PRINTS OF FASHION

NO. 2 – WALKING DRESS

A pelisse dress of autumnal brown sarsnet, made low in the neck, trimmed down the front and round the bottom with a rich trimming of vandyked white satin, ornamented with silver frogs; the sleeves buttoned on the inside of the arm, to correspond with the front of the dress; over the bosom is tied a light white net mantle, scalloped, and ornamented with acorn tassels. White satin bonnet, with a bunch of wheat in front, and short lace veil. Brown sandals and gloves. Green parasol.

Pelisse Dress of Autumn

Extract from
MANSFIELD PARK

Satisfied that the cause was now on a footing the most proper and hopeful, Sir Thomas resolved to abstain from all farther importunity with his niece, and to show no open interference. Upon her disposition he believed kindness might be the best way of working. Entreaty should be from one quarter only. The forbearance of her family on a point respecting which she could be in no doubt of their wishes might be their surest means of forwarding it. Accordingly, on this principle Sir Thomas took the first opportunity of saying to her, with a mild gravity intended to be overcoming, 'Well, Fanny, I have seen Mr Crawford again, and learn from him exactly how matters stand between you. He is a most extraordinary young man, and whatever be the event, you must feel that you have created an attachment of no common character; though, young as you are, and little acquainted with the transient, varying, unsteady nature of love as it generally exists, you cannot be struck as I am with all that is wonderful in a perseverance of this sort, against discouragement. With him, it is entirely a matter of feeling; he claims no merit in it, perhaps is entitled to none. Yet, having chosen so well, his constancy has a respectable stamp. Had his choice been less unexceptionable I should have condemned his persevering.'

'Indeed, Sir,' said Fanny, 'I am very sorry that Mr Crawford should continue to – I know that it is paying me a very great compliment, and I feel most undeservedly honoured, but I am so perfectly convinced, and I have told him so, that it never will be in my power –'

'My dear,' interrupted Sir Thomas, 'there is no occasion for this. Your feelings are as well known to me as my wishes and regrets must be to you. There is nothing more to be said or done. From this hour, the subject is never to be revived between us. You will have nothing to fear or to be agitated about. You cannot suppose me capable of trying to persuade you to marry against your inclinations. Your happiness and advantage are all that I have in view, and nothing is required of you but to bear with Mr Crawford's endeavours to convince you that they may not be incompatible with his. He proceeds at his own risk. You are on safe ground. I have engaged for your seeing him whenever he calls, as you might have done had nothing of this sort occurred. You will see him with the rest of us, in the same manner, and as much as you can, dismissing the recollection of everything unpleasant. He leaves Northamptonshire so soon, that even this slight sacrifice cannot be often demanded. The future must be very uncertain. And now, my dear Fanny, this subject is closed between us.'

The promised departure was all that Fanny could think of with much satisfaction. Her uncle's kind expressions, however, and forbearing manner, were sensibly felt; and when she considered how much of the truth was unknown to him, she believed she had no right to wonder at the line of conduct he pursued. He who had married a daughter to Mr Rushworth. Romantic delicacy was certainly not to be expected from him. She must do her duty and trust that time might make her duty easier than it now was.

She could not, though only eighteen, suppose Mr Crawford's

attachment would hold out for ever; she could not but imagine that steady, unceasing discouragement from herself would put an end to it in time. How much time she might, in her own fancy, allot for its dominion, is another concern. It would not be fair to enquire into a young lady's exact estimate of her own perfections.

In spite of his intended silence, Sir Thomas found himself once more obliged to mention the subject to his niece to prepare her briefly for its being imparted to her aunts; a measure which he would still have avoided, if possible, but which became necessary from the totally opposite feelings of Mr Crawford as to any secrecy of proceeding. He had no idea of concealment. It was all known at the Parsonage, where he loved to talk over the future with both his sisters; and it would be rather gratifying to him to have enlightened witnesses of the progress of his success. When Sir Thomas understood this, he felt the necessity of making his own wife and sister-in-law acquainted with the business without delay; though on Fanny's account he almost dreaded the effect of the communication to Mrs Norris as much as Fanny herself. He deprecated her mistaken, but well-meaning zeal. Sir Thomas, indeed, was, by this time, not very far from classing Mrs Norris as one of those well-meaning people who are always doing mistaken and very disagreeable things.

Mrs Norris, however, relieved him. He pressed for the strictest forbearance and silence towards their niece; she not only promised, but did observe it. She only looked her increased ill-will. Angry she was, bitterly angry; but she was more angry with Fanny for having received such an offer than for refusing it. It was an injury and affront to Julia, who ought to have been Mr Crawford's choice; and, independently of that, she disliked Fanny because she had neglected her; and she would have grudged such an elevation to one whom she had been always trying to depress.

Sir Thomas gave her more credit for discretion on the occasion than she deserved; and Fanny could have blessed her for allowing her only to see her displeasure, and not to hear it.

Lady Bertram took it differently. She had been a beauty, and a prosperous beauty, all her life; and beauty and wealth were all that excited her respect. To know Fanny to be sought in marriage by a man of fortune raised her, therefore, very much in her opinion. By convincing her that Fanny *was* very pretty, which she had been doubting about before, and that she would be advantageously married, it made her feel a sort of credit in calling her niece.

'Well, Fanny,' said she, as soon as they were alone together afterwards – and she really had known something like impatience to be alone with her, and her countenance, as she spoke, had extraordinary animation – 'Well, Fanny, I have had a very agreeable surprise this morning. I must just speak of it *once*, I told Sir Thomas I must *once*, and then I shall have done. I give you joy, my dear niece,' and looking at her complacently, she added 'Humph! We certainly are a handsome family.'

Fanny coloured, and doubted at first what to say; when hoping to assail her on her vulnerable side, she presently answered – 'My dear aunt, *you* cannot wish me to do differently from what I have done, I am sure. *You* cannot wish me to marry; for you would miss me, should not you? Yes, I am sure you would miss me too much for that.'

'No, my dear, I should not think of missing you when such an offer as this comes in your way. I could do very well without you if you were married to a man of such good estate as Mr Crawford.

And you must be aware, Fanny, that it is every young woman's duty to accept such a very unexceptionable offer as this.'

This was almost the only rule of conduct, the only piece of advice, which Fanny had ever received from her aunt in the course of eight years and a half. It silenced her. She felt how unprofitable contention would be. If her aunt's feelings were against her, nothing could be hoped from attacking her understanding. Lady Bertram was quite talkative.

'I will tell you what, Fanny,' said she. 'I am sure he fell in love with you at the ball, I am sure the mischief was done that evening. You did look remarkably well. Everybody said so. Sir Thomas said so. And you know you had Chapman to help you dress. I am very glad I sent Chapman to you. I shall tell Sir Thomas that I am sure it was done that evening.' And still pursuing the same cheerful thoughts, she soon afterwards added, 'And I will tell you what, Fanny – which is more than I did for Maria – the next time Pug has a litter you shall have a puppy.'

TAKING LIKENESSES

Jane Austen's art was one of 'taking likenesses', shrewdly observing the personalities of those around her and putting them into fiction. Emma Woodhouse is also an artist, a visual one, and Austen recognized a family resemblance when she is reported (by her nephew James Edward Austen) in his *Memoir* to have said Emma was 'a heroine whom no one but myself will much like'.

Emma takes a strong liking to Harriet Smith, a pretty parlour-boarder at the local school in Highbury, and tries to further Harriet's marriage prospects with the local vicar, Mr Elton. She takes his zealous prompting of her to paint Harriet's likeness to be an indication of his interest in Harriet, not recognizing that his compliments of her talent speak more to his ambitions to marry Emma herself.

Here we see a young lady in her 'morning' dress. 'Morning dress' designates clothing worn at the time of day before visiting, when women engaged in activities such as writing letters, taking breakfast or sketching. Dresses were customarily white, simply made and worn with the hair tied back; here, she wears a turban in fashionable imitation of 'oriental' styles and fabric (the muslin). There is a hint of hidden glamour in the clocks embroidered in lace on the stockings. Emma, too, plumps for glamour; she determines on a full-length watercolour for her obscure friend.

FASHIONS

FOR

MARCH, 1812

EXPLANATION OF THE PRINTS OF FASHION

NO. I – MORNING, OR HOME COSTUME

A white cambric frock, with a *demi-train*; short sleeves fastened up in front with cordon and tassels; a necklace formed of two rows of opal; the hair dressed in full curls, and confined by a demi turban of very fine muslin tied on the right side with a small bow; silk stockings with lace clocks, richly brocaded, and plain black kid slippers.

Morning, or Home Costume

Extract from
EMMA

'Did you ever have your likeness taken, Harriet?' said she: 'Did you ever sit for your picture?'

Harriet was on the point of leaving the room, and only stopped to say, with a very interesting naïveté, 'Oh! dear, no, never.'

No sooner was she out of sight, than Emma exclaimed, 'What an exquisite possession a good picture of her would be! I would give any money for it. I almost long to attempt her likeness myself. You do not know it I dare say, but two or three years ago I had a great passion for taking likenesses, and attempted several of my friends, and was thought to have a tolerable eye in general. But from one cause or another, I gave it up in disgust. But really, I could almost venture, if Harriet would sit to me. It would be such a delight to have her picture!'

'Let me entreat you,' cried Mr Elton; 'it would indeed be a delight! Let me entreat you, Miss Woodhouse, to exercise so charming a talent in favour of your friend. I know what your drawings are. How could you suppose me ignorant? Is not this room rich in specimens of your landscapes and flowers; and has not Mrs Weston some inimitable figure-pieces in her drawing-room at Randalls?'

Yes, good man! – thought Emma – but what has all that to do with taking likenesses? You know nothing of drawing. Don't pretend to be in raptures about mine. Keep your raptures for

Harriet's face. 'Well, if you give me such kind encouragement, Mr Elton, I believe I shall try what I can do. Harriet's features are very delicate, which makes a likeness difficult; and yet there is a peculiarity in the shape of the eye and the lines about the mouth which one ought to catch.'

'Exactly so – the shape of the eye and the lines about the mouth – I have not a doubt of your success. Pray, pray attempt it. As you will do it, it will indeed, to use your own words, be an exquisite possession.'

'But I am afraid, Mr Elton, Harriet will not like to sit. She thinks so little of her own beauty. Did not you observe her manner of answering me? How completely it meant, "why should my picture be drawn?"'

'Oh! yes, I observed it, I assure you. It was not lost on me. But still I cannot imagine she would not be persuaded.'

Harriet was soon back again, and the proposal almost immediately made; and she had no scruples which could stand many minutes against the earnest pressing of both the others. Emma wished to go to work directly, and therefore produced the portfolio containing her various attempts at portraits, for not one of them had ever been finished, that they might decide together on the best size for Harriet. Her many beginnings were displayed. Miniatures, half-lengths, whole-lengths, pencil, crayon, and watercolours had been all tried in turn. She had always wanted to do everything, and had made more progress both in drawing and music than many might have done with so little labour as she would ever submit to. She played and sang – and drew in almost every style; but steadiness had always been wanting; and in nothing had she approached the degree of excellence which she would have been glad to command, and ought not to have failed of. She was not much deceived as to her own skill either as an artist or a musician, but she was not unwilling to have others deceived, or sorry to know her reputation for accomplishment often higher than it deserved.

There was merit in every drawing – in the least finished, perhaps the most; her style was spirited; but had there been much less, or had there been ten times more, the delight and admiration of her two companions would have been the same. They were both in ecstasies. A likeness pleases everybody; and Miss Woodhouse's performances must be capital.

'No great variety of faces for you,' said Emma. 'I had only my own family to study from. There is my father – another of my father – but the idea of sitting for his picture made him so nervous, that I could only take him by stealth; neither of them very like, therefore. Mrs Weston again, and again, and again, you see. Dear Mrs Weston! always my kindest friend on every occasion. She would sit whenever I asked her. There is my sister; and really quite her own little elegant figure! – and the face not unlike. I should have made a good likeness of her, if she would have sat longer, but she was in such a hurry to have me draw her four children that she would not be quiet. Then, here come all my attempts at three of those four children – there they are, Henry and John and Bella, from one end of the sheet to the other, and any one of them might do for any one of the rest. She was so eager to have them drawn that I could not refuse; but there is no making children of three or four years old stand still, you know; nor can it be very easy to take any likeness of them, beyond the air and complexion, unless they are coarser featured than any mamma's children ever were. Here is my sketch of the fourth, who was a baby. I took him, as he was sleeping on the sofa, and it is as strong a likeness of his cockade as you would wish to see. He had nestled down his head most conveniently. That's very like. I am rather proud of little George. The corner of the sofa is very good. Then here is my last' – unclosing a pretty sketch of a gentleman in small size, whole-length – 'my last and my best – my brother, Mr John Knightley – This did not want much of being finished, when I put it away in a pet, and vowed I would never take another likeness. I could not help being provoked; for after all my pains, and when I had really made a very good likeness of it – (Mrs Weston and I were quite agreed in thinking it *very* like) – only too handsome – too flattering – but that was a fault on the right side – after all this, came poor dear Isabella's cold approbation of – "Yes, it was a little like – but to be sure it did not do him justice." We had had a great deal of trouble in persuading him to sit at all. It was made a great favour of; and altogether it was more than I could bear; and so I never would finish it, to have it apologised over as an unfavourable likeness, to every morning visitor in Brunswick Square – and, as I said, I did then forswear ever drawing anybody again. But for Harriet's sake, or rather for my own, and as there are no husbands and wives in the case at present, I will break my resolution now.'

Mr Elton seemed very properly struck and delighted by the idea, and was repeating, 'No husbands and wives in the case *at present*, indeed, as you observe. Exactly so. No husbands and wives,' with so interesting a consciousness, that Emma began to consider whether she had not better leave them together at once. But as she wanted to be drawing, the declaration must wait a little longer.

She had soon fixed on the size and sort of portrait. It was to be a whole-length in watercolours, like Mr John Knightley's, and was destined, if she could please herself, to hold a very honourable station over the mantelpiece.

CHRISTMAS CARRIAGES

Jane Austen was a December baby. Emma, who may have been a secret favourite heroine of the author, undergoes a significant challenge in the same month.

A snowy Christmas party on Christmas Eve 1813 is a centrepiece in the heroine's slow discovery of the wrongheadedness of her imperious imagination. The Woodhouse party are anxious to get home to Hartfield when snow settles at the party. In the flurry to board carriages, Emma finds herself alone in a carriage with a somewhat sozzled Mr Elton, who proceeds, to her horror, to embark on an unexpected proposal.

Since her heroine is a wealthy, young and lovely heiress, Austen might have imagined Emma clad in an ensemble not unlike that shown in our illustration for a wintry carriage ride. The pelisse (long coat) in a bright red is trimmed with ermine and topped with a jaunty hat also in fur. Mancheron (the word from the French) sleeves have a piece of trimming on the upper part of the shoulder. Military masculine styles remained in vogue for carriage and travelling dress throughout the period of the Napoleonic Wars (1803–1815). The large fur muff to keep the hands warm in a chilly carriage is also positioned defensively in front of the body, which is appropriate given the threat of amorous assault in this scene from *Emma*.

FASHIONS

FOR

JANUARY, 1817

EXPLANATION OF THE PRINTS OF FASHION

ENGLISH

NO. 2 — CARRIAGE COSTUME

A velvet pelisse of a bright carmine red, superbly trimmed with ermine; the tops of the sleeves caught up *à-la-Mancheron*, with rich military silk chain work, the colour of the pelisse. Russian hussar cap of ermine, ornamented with gold military chain. Limerick gloves and half-boots or shoes of kid, of a correspondent colour.

Carriage Costume

Extract from

EMMA

She had not time to know how Mr Elton took the reproof, so rapidly did another subject succeed; for Mr John Knightley now came into the room from examining the weather, and opened on them all with the information of the ground being covered with snow, and of its still snowing fast, with a strong drifting wind; concluding with these words to Mr Woodhouse – 'This will prove a spirited beginning of your winter engagements, sir. Something new for your coachman and horses to be making their way through a storm of snow.'

Poor Mr Woodhouse was silent from consternation; but everybody else had something to say; everybody was either surprised or not surprised, and had some question to ask, or some comfort to offer. Mrs Weston and Emma tried earnestly to cheer him and turn his attention from his son-in-law, who was pursuing his triumph rather unfeelingly.

'I admired your resolution very much, sir,' said he, 'in venturing out in such weather, for of course you saw there would be snow very soon. Everybody must have seen the snow coming on. I admired your spirit; and I dare say we shall get home very well. Another hour or two's snow can hardly make the road impassable; and we are two carriages; if *one* is blown over in the bleak part of the common field there will be the other at hand. I dare say we shall be all safe at Hartfield before midnight.'

Mr Weston, with triumph of a different sort, was confessing

Is this fair, Mrs Weston?

that he had known it to be snowing some time, but had not said a word, lest it should make Mr Woodhouse uncomfortable, and be an excuse for his hurrying away. As to there being any quantity of snow fallen or likely to fall to impede their return, that was a mere joke; he was afraid they would find no difficulty. He wished the road might be impassable, that he might be able to keep them all at Randalls; and with the utmost goodwill was sure that accommodation might be found for everybody, calling on his wife to agree with him, that, with a little contrivance, everybody might be lodged, which she hardly knew how to do, from the consciousness of there being but two spare rooms in the house.

'What is to be done, my dear Emma? – what is to be done?' was Mr Woodhouse's first exclamation, and all that he could say for some time. To her he looked for comfort; and her assurances of safety, her representation of the excellence of the horses, and of James, and of their having so many friends about them, revived him a little.

His eldest daughter's alarm was equal to his own. The horror of being blocked up at Randalls, while her children were at Hartfield, was full in her imagination; and fancying the road to be now just passable for adventurous people, but in a state that admitted no delay, she was eager to have it settled, that her father and Emma should remain at Randalls, while she and her husband set forward instantly through all the possible accumulations of drifted snow that might impede them.

'You had better order the carriage directly, my love,' said she; 'I dare say we shall be able to get along, if we set off directly; and if we do come to any thing very bad, I can get out and walk. I am not at all afraid. I should not mind walking half the way. I could change my shoes, you know, the moment I got home; and it is not the sort of thing that gives me cold.'

'Indeed!' replied he. 'Then, my dear Isabella, it is the most extraordinary sort of thing in the world, for in general everything does give you cold. Walk home! – you are prettily shod for walking home, I dare say. It will be bad enough for the horses.'

Isabella turned to Mrs Weston for her approbation of the plan. Mrs Weston could only approve. Isabella then went to Emma; but Emma could not so entirely give up the hope of their being all able to get away; and they were still discussing the point, when Mr Knightley, who had left the room immediately after his brother's first report of the snow, came back again, and told them that he had been out of doors to examine, and could answer for there not being the smallest difficulty in their getting home, whenever they liked it, either now or an hour hence. He had gone beyond the sweep – some way along the Highbury road – the snow was no where above half an inch deep – in many places hardly enough to whiten the ground; a very few flakes were falling at present, but the clouds were parting, and there was every appearance of its being soon over. He had seen the coachmen, and they both agreed with him in there being nothing to apprehend.

To Isabella, the relief of such tidings was very great, and they were scarcely less acceptable to Emma on her father's account, who was immediately set as much at ease on the subject as his nervous constitution allowed; but the alarm that had been raised could not be appeased so as to admit of any comfort for him while he continued at Randalls. He was satisfied of there being no present danger in returning home, but no assurances could convince him that it was safe to stay; and while the others were variously urging and recommending, Mr Knightley and Emma settled it in a few brief sentences: thus – 'Your father will not be easy; why do not you go?'

'I am ready, if the others are.'

'Shall I ring the bell?'

'Yes, do.'

And the bell was rung, and the carriages spoken for. A few minutes more, and Emma hoped to see one troublesome companion deposited in his own house, to get sober and cool, and the other recover his temper and happiness when this visit of hardship were over.

The carriages came: and Mr Woodhouse, always the first object on such occasions, was carefully attended to his own by Mr Knightley and Mr Weston; but not all that either could say could prevent some renewal of alarm at the sight of the snow which had actually fallen, and the discovery of a much darker night than he had been prepared for. 'He was afraid they should have a very bad drive. He was afraid poor Isabella would not like it. And there would be poor Emma in the carriage behind. He did not know what they had best do. They must keep as much together as they could;' and James was talked to, and given a charge to go very slow and wait for the other carriage.

Isabella stepped in after her father; John Knightley, forgetting that he did not belong to their party, stepped in after his wife very naturally; so that Emma found, on being escorted and followed into the second carriage by Mr Elton, that the door was to be lawfully shut on them, and that they were to have a tête-a-tête drive. It would not have been the awkwardness of a moment, it would have been rather a pleasure, previous to the suspicions of this very day; she could have talked to him of Harriet, and the three-quarters of a mile would have seemed but one. But now, she would rather it had not happened. She believed he had been drinking too much of Mr Weston's good wine, and felt sure that he would want to be talking nonsense.

To restrain him as much as might be, by her own manners, she was immediately preparing to speak with exquisite calmness and gravity of the weather and the night; but scarcely had she begun, scarcely had they passed the sweep-gate and joined the other carriage, than she found her subject cut up – her hand seized – her attention demanded, and Mr Elton actually making violent love to her: availing himself of the precious opportunity, declaring sentiments which must be already well known, hoping – fearing – adoring – ready to die if she refused him; but flattering himself that his ardent attachment and unequalled love and unexampled passion could not fail of having some effect, and in short, very much resolved on being seriously accepted as soon as possible. It really was so. Without scruple – without apology – without much apparent diffidence, Mr Elton, the lover of Harriet, was professing himself *her* lover. She tried to stop him; but vainly; he would go on, and say it all.

ALLIES AND ENEMIES

In *Emma* (1815), a ball, fraught with romantic cross-currents, social snubs and kind gestures, is held one May evening in 1814 at the Crown Inn in Highbury. Emma's eyes are on George Knightley, who is standing slightly apart from the dancing.

Her attention is diverted when she sees newly-married and fiercely ambitious Mr Elton – still smarting from Emma's rejection of his proposal and the revelation that Emma had thought lowly Harriet Smith might make him a suitable bride – cruelly snub partnerless Harriet in public. Mr Knightley gallantly steps in to lead poor Harriet into the couples.

The micropolitics of this ball suggest the politics of enmity and alliance in Europe. In June 1813, Arthur Wellesley, Duke of Wellington, had personally led an army to victory against the French at Vitoria. The Russian emperor Alexander and his allies (Britain, Austria, Prussia) had marched into Paris on 31 March 1814, forcing Napoleon to abdicate. On 20 April, Napoleon bade farewell to his troops and set out for exile on Elba. Wellington was treated as a hero. Celebrations were held across the country and *La Belle Assemblée*, always up to date, suggested appropriate fashions for balls in June of 1814. The pink and white ball dress is appropriately topped with a 'Wellington' laurel wreath in white or green foil.

FASHIONS

FOR
JUNE, 1814

EXPLANATION OF THE PRINTS OF FASHION

NO. I – BALL DRESS FOR THE FETES IN HONOUR OF THE EMPEROR OF RUSSIA AND THE ALLIES

White lace drapery over a pale pink satin slip; the drapery is trimmed round with scollops, which are edged with narrow blond lace, put on very full, and is rather shorter than the slip, which is also edged with blond. A pink satin body is worn over the drapery; the back is made tight to the shape, and is finished behind in a point to correspond with the front; the back is the same breadth as last month, but unusually high. Fancy sleeve. Scollops of lace edged with blond falls over the neck, and is edged to correspond with the train. The points of the body are ornamented with pearl *fleur de lys*, which have most tasteful effect. Pearl necklace, bracelets, earrings, and armlets; locket, intermingled pearls and coloured stones. Head-dress the Wellington wreath of laurel in white or green foil, interspersed with regal crowns and other applicable attributes: it is a most elegant, novel, and tasteful ornament for any full head-dress whatever, and at this period should be universally worn. White kid slippers and gloves.

Ball Dress for the Fetes in honour of the Emperor of Russia and the Allies

Extract from

EMMA

Emma was smiling with enjoyment, delighted to see the respectable length of the set as it was forming, and to feel that she had so many hours of unusual festivity before her – She was more disturbed by Mr Knightley's not dancing, than by anything else. There he was, among the standers-by, where he ought not to be; he ought to be dancing – not classing himself with the husbands, and fathers, and whist-players, who were pretending to feel an interest in the dance till their rubbers were made up – so young as he looked! – He could not have appeared to greater advantage perhaps anywhere, than where he had placed himself. His tall, firm, upright figure, among the bulky forms and stooping shoulders of the elderly men, was such as Emma felt must draw everybody's eyes; and, excepting her own partner, there was not one among the whole row of young men who could be compared with him – He moved a few steps nearer, and those few steps were enough to prove in how gentlemanlike a manner, with what natural grace, he must have danced, would he but take the trouble – Whenever she caught his eye, she forced him to smile; but in general he was looking grave. She wished he could love a ballroom better, and could like Frank Churchill better – He seemed often observing her. She must not flatter herself that he thought of her dancing; but if he were criticising her behaviour, she did not feel afraid. There was nothing like flirtation between her and her partner. They seemed more like cheerful, easy friends, than lovers. That Frank Churchill thought less of her than he had done, was indubitable.

The ball proceeded pleasantly. The anxious cares, the incessant attentions of Mrs Weston, were not thrown away. Everybody seemed happy; and the praise of being a delightful ball, which is seldom bestowed till after a ball has ceased to be, was repeatedly given in the very beginning of the existence of this. Of very important, very recordable events, it was not more productive than such meetings usually are. There was one, however, which Emma thought something of – The two last dances before supper were begun, and Harriet had no partner – the only young lady sitting down – and so equal had been hitherto the number of dancers, that how there could be anyone disengaged was the wonder! – But Emma's wonder lessened soon afterwards, on seeing Mr Elton sauntering about. He would not ask Harriet to dance if it were possible to be avoided: she was sure he would not – and she was expecting him every moment to escape into the card-room.

Escape, however, was not his plan. He came to the part of the room where the sitters-by were collected, spoke to some, and walked about in front of them, as if to show his liberty, and his resolution of maintaining it. He did not omit being sometimes directly before Miss Smith, or speaking to those who were close to her. Emma saw it. She was not yet dancing; she was working her way up from the bottom, and had therefore leisure to look around, and by only turning her head a little she saw it all. When she was halfway up the set, the whole group were exactly behind her, and she would no longer allow her eyes to watch; but Mr Elton was so near, that she heard every syllable of a dialogue which just then took place between him and Mrs Weston; and she perceived that his wife, who was standing immediately above

Among the bulky forms and stooping shoulders

her, was not only listening also, but even encouraging him by significant glances – The kind-hearted, gentle Mrs Weston had left her seat to join him and say, 'Do not you dance, Mr Elton?' to which his prompt reply was, 'Most readily, Mrs Weston, if you will dance with me.'

'Me! – oh! no – I would get you a better partner than myself. I am no dancer.'

'If Mrs Gilbert wishes to dance,' said he, 'I shall have great pleasure, I am sure – for, though beginning to feel myself rather an old married man, and that my dancing days are over, it would give me very great pleasure at any time to stand up with an old friend like Mrs Gilbert.'

'Mrs Gilbert does not mean to dance, but there is a young lady disengaged whom I should be very glad to see dancing – Miss Smith.' 'Miss Smith! – oh! – I had not observed. You are extremely obliging – and if I were not an old married man – But my dancing days are over, Mrs Weston. You will excuse me. Anything else I should be most happy to do, at your command – but my dancing days are over.'

Mrs Weston said no more; and Emma could imagine with what surprise and mortification she must be returning to her seat. This was Mr Elton! the amiable, obliging, gentle Mr Elton – She looked round for a moment; he had joined Mr Knightley at a little distance, and was arranging himself for settled conversation, while smiles of high glee passed between him and his wife.

She would not look again. Her heart was in a glow, and she feared her face might be as hot.

In another moment a happier sight caught her – Mr Knightley leading Harriet to the set! – Never had she been more surprised, seldom more delighted, than at that instant. She was all pleasure and gratitude, both for Harriet and herself, and longed to be thanking him; and though too distant for speech, her countenance said much, as soon as she could catch his eye again.

His dancing proved to be just what she had believed it, extremely good; and Harriet would have seemed almost too lucky, if it had not been for the cruel state of things before, and for the very complete enjoyment and very high sense of the distinction which her happy features announced. It was not thrown away on her, she bounded higher than ever, flew farther down the middle, and was in a continual course of smiles.

Mr Elton had retreated into the cardroom, looking (Emma trusted) very foolish. She did not think he was quite so hardened as his wife, though growing very like her – *she* spoke some of her feelings, by observing audibly to her partner, 'Knightley has taken pity on poor little Miss Smith! – Very good-natured, I declare.'

FALLING AT LYME

Persuasion was the last full novel by Jane Austen; it was completed on 6 August 1816 but not published until 20 December 1817, five months after her death from an illness that remains undiagnosed. It is a mature work that readers come to love more on each reading.

Anne Elliot, the loveable heroine her author described in a letter as 'almost too good for me', meets and loves all over again the suitor Captain Frederick Wentworth, whom she was persuaded not to marry over seven years previously.

An especially powerful scene takes place in the coastal resort of Lyme Regis, Dorset, to which Anne Elliot travels for a two-day visit with her younger sister Mary Musgrove, Mary's husband Charles and his sisters, Louisa and Henrietta. Captain Wentworth is also with them and Anne is heartsore as she watches Wentworth's attentions to extroverted and impulsive Louisa Musgrove. It is windy, Louisa insists on jumping from the steps of the harbour wall into the arms of Frederick below and there is a terrible accident when she jumps too early.

Our illustration shows a lady 'of rank', all her frills and furbelows wind-tossed at another coastal resort – Brighton in East Sussex. With a telescope pressed to her eye, she looks out to sea, at the uncertain future that *Persuasion* has Anne Elliot commit to all those years after her wrong decision.

FASHIONS

FOR

OCTOBER, 1809

EXPLANATION OF THE PRINTS OF FASHION

ENGLISH COSTUME

A DRESS WORN BY A LADY OF RANK ON THE STEINE AT BRIGHTON

A bonnet composed of yellow satin and lace, richly embossed with leopard spots in deep orange; the front in the tiara form, bound with green figured ribband; a band of the same confines the crown, and ties in a bow behind; a long veil thrown back; a robe of yellow craped muslin, made to sit tight to the figure, confined at the bosom and down the front with knots of green ribband, bound round the neck and ornamented round the bottom with three rows of the same; long sleeves, with small lace ruffles hemmed to correspond; a high lace tucker, fastened on the bosom with an Egyptian pebble. A zephyr cloak of rich lace, falling in long points to the feet, finished with silk tassels, sloped up in the form of a jacket behind, meeting at the bosom and on the shoulders, confined with graceful negligence to the form by a sash of green ribband. Yellow Morocco sandals; gloves of York tan.

A Sea Coast Promenade Fashion

Extract from

PERSUASION

Breakfast had not been long over, when they were joined by Captain and Mrs Harville and Captain Benwick; with whom they had appointed to take their last walk about Lyme. They ought to be setting off for Uppercross by one, and in the meanwhile were to be all together, and out of doors as long as they could.

Anne found Captain Benwick getting near her, as soon as they were all fairly in the street. Their conversation the preceding evening did not disincline him to seek her again; and they walked together some time, talking as before of Mr Scott and Lord Byron, and still as unable as before, and as unable as any other two readers, to think exactly alike of the merits of either, till something occasioned an almost general change amongst their party, and instead of Captain Benwick, she had Captain Harville by her side.

'Miss Elliot,' said he, speaking rather low, 'you have done a good deed in making that poor fellow talk so much. I wish he could have such company oftener. It is bad for him, I know, to be shut up as he is; but what can we do? We cannot part.'

'No,' said Anne, 'that I can easily believe to be impossible; but in time, perhaps – we know what time does in every case of affliction, and you must remember, Captain Harville, that your friend may yet be called a young mourner – only last summer, I understand.'

'Ay, true enough,' (with a deep sigh) 'only June.'

'And not known to him, perhaps, so soon.'

'Not till the first week of August, when he came home from the Cape, just made into the *Grappler*. I was at Plymouth dreading to hear of him; he sent in letters, but the *Grappler* was under orders for Portsmouth. There the news must follow him, but who was to tell it? Not I. I would as soon have been run up to the yardarm. Nobody could do it, but that good fellow' (pointing to Captain Wentworth). 'The *Laconia* had come into Plymouth the week before; no danger of her being sent to sea again. He stood his chance for the rest; wrote up for leave of absence, but without waiting the return, travelled night and day till he got to Portsmouth, rowed off to the *Grappler* that instant, and never left the poor fellow for a week. That's what he did, and nobody else could have saved poor James. You may think, Miss Elliot, whether he is dear to us!'

Anne did think on the question with perfect decision, and said as much in reply as her own feeling could accomplish, or as his seemed able to bear, for he was too much affected to renew the subject, and when he spoke again, it was of something totally different.

Mrs Harville's giving it as her opinion that her husband would have quite walking enough by the time he reached home, determined the direction of all the party in what was to be their last walk; they would accompany them to their door, and then return and set off themselves. By all their calculations there was just time for this; but as they drew near the Cobb, there was such a general wish to walk along it once more, all were so inclined, and Louisa soon grew so determined, that the difference of a quarter of an hour, it was found, would be no difference at all; so with all the kind leave-taking, and all the kind interchange of invitations and promises which may be imagined, they parted from Captain and Mrs Harville at their own door, and still accompanied by Captain Benwick, who seemed to cling to them to the last, proceeded to make the proper adieus to the Cobb.

Anne found Captain Benwick again drawing near her. Lord Byron's 'dark blue seas' could not fail of being brought forward by their present view, and she gladly gave him all her attention as long as attention was possible. It was soon drawn, perforce another way.

There was too much wind to make the high part of the new Cobb pleasant for the ladies, and they agreed to get down the steps to the lower, and all were contented to pass quietly and carefully down the steep flight, excepting Louisa; she must be jumped down them by Captain Wentworth. In all their walks, he had had to jump her from the stiles; the sensation was delightful to her. The hardness of the pavement for her feet, made him less willing upon the present occasion; he did it, however. She was safely down, and instantly, to show her enjoyment, ran up the steps to be jumped down again. He advised her against it, thought the jar too great; but no, he reasoned and talked in vain, she smiled and said, 'I am determined I will;' he put out his hands; she was too precipitate by half a second, she fell on the pavement on the Lower Cobb, and was taken up lifeless! There was no wound, no blood, no visible bruise; but her eyes were closed, she breathed not, her face was like death. The horror of the moment to all who stood around!

Captain Wentworth, who had caught her up, knelt with her in his arms, looking on her with a face as pallid as her own, in an agony of silence. 'She is dead! she is dead!' screamed Mary, catching hold of her husband, and contributing with his own horror to make him immoveable; and in another moment, Henrietta, sinking under the conviction, lost her senses too, and would have fallen on the steps, but for Captain Benwick and Anne, who caught and supported her between them.

'Is there no one to help me?' were the first words which burst from Captain Wentworth, in a tone of despair, and as if all his own strength were gone.

'Go to him, go to him,' cried Anne, 'for heaven's sake go to him. I can support her myself. Leave me, and go to him. Rub her hands, rub her temples; here are salts; take them, take them.'

Captain Benwick obeyed, and Charles at the same moment, disengaging himself from his wife, they were both with him; and Louisa was raised up and supported more firmly between them, and everything was done that Anne had prompted, but in vain; while Captain Wentworth, staggering against the wall for his support, exclaimed in the bitterest agony, 'Oh God! her father and mother!'

'A surgeon!' said Anne.

He caught the word; it seemed to rouse him at once, and saying only – 'True, true, a surgeon this instant,' was darting away, when Anne eagerly suggested, 'Captain Benwick, would not it be better for Captain Benwick? He knows where a surgeon is to be found.'

Everyone capable of thinking felt the advantage of the idea, and in a moment (it was all done in rapid moments) Captain Benwick had resigned the poor corpse-like figure entirely to the brother's care, and was off for the town with the utmost rapidity.

As to the wretched party left behind, it could scarcely be said which of the three, who were completely rational, was suffering most: Captain Wentworth, Anne, or Charles, who, really a very affectionate brother, hung over Louisa with sobs of grief, and could only turn his eyes from one sister, to see the other in a state

Looking on her with a face as pallid as her own

as insensible, or to witness the hysterical agitations of his wife, calling on him for help which he could not give.

Anne, attending with all the strength and zeal, and thought, which instinct supplied, to Henrietta, still tried, at intervals, to suggest comfort to the others, tried to quiet Mary, to animate Charles, to assuage the feelings of Captain Wentworth. Both seemed to look to her for directions.

'Anne, Anne,' cried Charles, 'What is to be done next? What, in heaven's name, is to be done next?'

Captain Wentworth's eyes were also turned towards her.

'Had not she better be carried to the inn? Yes, I am sure: carry her gently to the inn.'

'Yes, yes, to the inn,' repeated Captain Wentworth, comparatively collected, and eager to be doing something. 'I will carry her myself. Musgrove, take care of the others.'

By this time the report of the accident had spread among the workmen and boatmen about the Cobb, and many were collected near them, to be useful if wanted, at any rate, to enjoy the sight of a dead young lady, nay, two dead young ladies, for it proved twice as fine as the first report. To some of the best-looking of these good people Henrietta was consigned, for, though partially revived, she was quite helpless; and in this manner, Anne walking by her side, and Charles attending to his wife, they set forward, treading back with feelings unutterable, the ground, which so lately, so very lately, and so light of heart, they had passed along.

They were not off the Cobb before the Harvilles met them. Captain Benwick had been seen flying by their house, with a countenance which showed something to be wrong; and they had set off immediately, informed and directed as they passed, towards the spot. Shocked as Captain Harville was, he brought senses and nerves that could be instantly useful; and a look between him and his wife decided what was to be done. She must be taken to their house; all must go to their house; and await the surgeon's arrival there. They would not listen to scruples: he was obeyed; they were all beneath his roof; and while Louisa, under Mrs Harville's direction, was conveyed upstairs and given possession of her own bed, assistance, cordials, restoratives were supplied by her husband to all who needed them.

Louisa had once opened her eyes, but soon closed them again, without apparent consciousness. This had been a proof of life, however, of service to her sister; and Henrietta, though perfectly incapable of being in the same room with Louisa, was kept, by the agitation of hope and fear, from a return of her own insensibility. Mary, too, was growing calmer.

The surgeon was with them almost before it had seemed possible. They were sick with horror, while he examined; but he was not hopeless. The head had received a severe contusion, but he had seen greater injuries recovered from: he was by no means hopeless; he spoke cheerfully.

That he did not regard it as a desperate case, that he did not say a few hours must end it, was at first felt, beyond the hope of most; and the ecstasy of such a reprieve, the rejoicing, deep and silent, after a few fervent ejaculations of gratitude to Heaven had been offered, may be conceived.

The tone, the look, with which 'Thank God!' was uttered by Captain Wentworth, Anne was sure could never be forgotten by her; nor the sight of him afterwards, as he sat near a table, leaning over it with folded arms and face concealed, as if overpowered by the various feelings of his soul, and trying by prayer and reflection to calm them.

Louisa's limbs had escaped. There was no injury but to the head.

CONCERTED EFFORTS

In the concluding scenes of *Persuasion* (1817), Anne Elliot attends a concert in Bath and her feelings – as she comes to realize that Frederick Wentworth's love has returned to her – are intense and minutely detailed.

Anne is a musician, accomplished on the pianoforte. Her sensitivity to sound and vibration is not only technical – as we see when she explains to her cousin Mr Elliot the meaning of the Italian words to a song – but also emotional: she recognizes that Wentworth is jealous. The scene is dynamically scored by an author at the height of her powers.

Appropriately, our illustration recommends 'Full Dress for the Opera, Theatre &c.' The design and explanation both come from the indefatigable Mary Ann Bell, daughter-in-law to the journal's owner, John Bell. The full dress is topped with a 'Britannia toque', a turban-like hat on which she confers a name that doffs to recent victories against Napoleon. That the ensemble is designed for a music concert, the theatre, or dining, rather than a ball, is indicated by the relatively high neck and long sleeves. But the glowing ruby velvet, the careful shaping of the gown to the chest, Mary Ann insists, suggest novelty, elegance and taste, qualities that Anne Elliot's suitors recognize in her.

FASHIONS

FOR

MARCH, 1815

EXPLANATION OF THE PRINTS OF FASHION

NO. 2 – DINNER DRESS

A short round dress of bright ruby velvet, or twilled sarsnet; if the latter it should be shot with white. The form of this dress is extremely novel and elegant; the body, which is formed in the frock style, is calculated to display the beauty of the chest to the utmost advantage; and to such ladies as are not peculiarly well formed about the bosom it gives an appearance of width to the chest, as well as an easy elegance to the shape, which must be seen to be credited. Long sleeve, composed of white lace, made, as all the sleeves of the present month are, very full, the fullness is drawn in at the top in the front of the arm, and it is confined at the wrist in a novel and tasteful style. White lace French tucker, which we have no hesitation in saying is by far the most elegant thing that has been introduced for a length of time and does the highest credit to the taste and inventiveness of Mrs. Bell; it is so contrived as to shade the bosom while it leaves that part of the neck bare which may be exposed without indelicacy; it finishes the dress in a style the most chaste, novel and tasteful that we have ever seen. The bottom of the dress is simply ornamented with two rows of bias lace or crape, put on the reverse way, and lightly finished round the edge with a French beading. Head-dress, the Britannia Toque, composed of ruby velvet, and finished with a gold or silver band and a white ostrich feather. This cap which is rather in the French style, is elegantly appropriate to dinner dress. White kid slippers and gloves; small ivory French fan.

The above dresses were invented by Mrs. Bell, Inventress of the Ladies *Chapeau Bras* and the Circassian Corsets, and of whom only they can be had, at her *Magazin des Modes*, No. 26, Charlotte Street, Bedfordshire.

Full Dress for the Opera, Theatre &c.

Extract from

PERSUASION

As she ceased, the entrance door opened again, and the very party appeared for whom they were waiting. 'Lady Dalrymple, Lady Dalrymple,' was the rejoicing sound; and with all the eagerness compatible with anxious elegance, Sir Walter and his two ladies stepped forward to meet her. Lady Dalrymple and Miss Carteret, escorted by Mr Elliot and Colonel Wallis, who had happened to arrive nearly at the same instant, advanced into the room. The others joined them, and it was a group in which Anne found herself also necessarily included. She was divided from Captain Wentworth. Their interesting, almost too interesting conversation must be broken up for a time, but slight was the penance compared with the happiness which brought it on! She had learnt, in the last ten minutes, more of his feelings towards Louisa, more of all his feelings than she dared to think of; and she gave herself up to the demands of the party, to the needful civilities of the moment, with exquisite, though agitated sensations. She was in good humour with all. She had received ideas which disposed her to be courteous and kind to all, and to pity everyone, as being less happy than herself.

The delightful emotions were a little subdued, when, on stepping back from the group, to be joined again by Captain Wentworth, she saw that he was gone. She was just in time to see him turn into the Concert Room. He was gone; he had disappeared; she felt a moment's regret. But 'they should meet again. He would look for her, he would find her out before the evening were over, and at present, perhaps, it was as well to be asunder. She was in need of a little interval for recollection.'

Upon Lady Russell's appearance soon afterwards, the whole party was collected, and all that remained was to marshal themselves, and proceed into the Concert Room; and be of all the consequence in their power, draw as many eyes, excite as many whispers, and disturb as many people as they could.

Very, very happy were both Elizabeth and Anne Elliot as they walked in. Elizabeth arm in arm with Miss Carteret, and looking on the broad back of the dowager Viscountess Dalrymple before her, had nothing to wish for which did not seem within her reach; and Anne – but it would be an insult to the nature of Anne's felicity, to draw any comparison between it and her sister's: the origin of one all selfish vanity, of the other all generous attachment.

Anne saw nothing, thought nothing of the brilliancy of the room. Her happiness was from within. Her eyes were bright and her cheeks glowed; but she knew nothing about it. She was thinking only of the last half-hour, and as they passed to their seats, her mind took a hasty range over it. His choice of subjects, his expressions, and still more his manner and look, had been such as she could see in only one light. His opinion of Louisa Musgrove's inferiority, an opinion which he had seemed solicitous to give, his wonder at Captain Benwick, his feelings as to a first, strong attachment; sentences begun which he could not finish, his half-averted eyes and more than half-expressive glance, all, all declared that he had a heart returning to her at least; that anger, resentment, avoidance, were no more; and that they were succeeded, not merely by friendship and regard, but by the tenderness of the past. Yes, some share of the tenderness

With all the eagerness compatible with anxious elegance

of the past. She could not contemplate the change as implying less. He must love her.

These were thoughts, with their attendant visions, which occupied and flurried her too much to leave her any power of observation; and she passed along the room without having a glimpse of him, without even trying to discern him. When their places were determined on, and they were all properly arranged, she looked round to see if he should happen to be in the same part of the room, but he was not; her eye could not reach him; and the concert being just opening, she must consent for a time to be happy in a humbler way.

The party was divided and disposed of on two contiguous benches: Anne was among those on the foremost, and Mr Elliot had manoeuvred so well, with the assistance of his friend Colonel Wallis, as to have a seat by her. Miss Elliot, surrounded by her cousins, and the principal object of Colonel Wallis's gallantry, was quite contented.

Anne's mind was in a most favourable state for the entertainment of the evening; it was just occupation enough: she had feelings for the tender, spirits for the gay, attention for the scientific, and patience for the wearisome; and had never liked a concert better, at least during the first act. Towards the close of it, in the interval succeeding an Italian song, she explained the words of the song to Mr Elliot. They had a concert bill between them.

'This,' said she, 'is nearly the sense, or rather the meaning of the words, for certainly the sense of an Italian love-song must not be talked of, but it is as nearly the meaning as I can give; for I do not pretend to understand the language. I am a very poor Italian scholar.'

'Yes, yes, I see you are. I see you know nothing of the matter.

You have only knowledge enough of the language to translate at sight these inverted, transposed, curtailed Italian lines, into clear, comprehensible, elegant English. You need not say anything more of your ignorance. Here is complete proof.'

'I will not oppose such kind politeness; but I should be sorry to be examined by a real proficient.'

'I have not had the pleasure of visiting in Camden Place so long,' replied he, 'without knowing something of Miss Anne Elliot; and I do regard her as one who is too modest for the world in general to be aware of half her accomplishments, and too highly accomplished for modesty to be natural in any other woman.'

'For shame! for shame! this is too much flattery. I forget what we are to have next,' turning to the bill.

'Perhaps,' said Mr Elliot, speaking low, 'I have had a longer acquaintance with your character than you are aware of.'

'Indeed! How so? You can have been acquainted with it only since I came to Bath, excepting as you might hear me previously spoken of in my own family.'

'I knew you by report long before you came to Bath. I had heard you described by those who knew you intimately. I have been acquainted with you by character many years. Your person, your disposition, accomplishments, manner; they were all present to me.'

Mr Elliot was not disappointed in the interest he hoped to raise. No one can withstand the charm of such a mystery. To have been described long ago to a recent acquaintance, by nameless people, is irresistible; and Anne was all curiosity. She wondered, and questioned him eagerly: but in vain. He delighted in being asked, but he would not tell.

'No, no, some time or other, perhaps, but not now. He would

mention no names now; but such, he could assure her, had been the fact. He had many years ago received such a description of Miss Anne Elliot as had inspired him with the highest idea of her merit, and excited the warmest curiosity to know her.'

Anne could think of no one so likely to have spoken with partiality of her many years ago as the Mr Wentworth of Monkford, Captain Wentworth's brother. He might have been in Mr Elliot's company, but she had not courage to ask the question.

'The name of Anne Elliot,' said he, 'has long had an interesting sound to me. Very long has it possessed a charm over my fancy; and, if I dared, I would breathe my wishes that the name might never change.'

Such, she believed, were his words; but scarcely had she received their sound, than her attention was caught by other sounds immediately behind her, which rendered everything else trivial. Her father and Lady Dalrymple were speaking.

'A well-looking man,' said Sir Walter, 'a very well-looking man.'

'A very fine young man indeed!' said Lady Dalrymple. 'More air than one often sees in Bath. Irish, I dare say.'

'No, I just know his name. A bowing acquaintance. Wentworth; Captain Wentworth of the navy. His sister married my tenant in Somersetshire, the Croft, who rents Kellynch.'

Before Sir Walter had reached this point, Anne's eyes had caught the right direction, and distinguished Captain Wentworth standing among a cluster of men at a little distance. As her eyes fell on him, his seemed to be withdrawn from her. It had that appearance. It seemed as if she had been one moment too late; and as long as she dared observe, he did not look again; but the performance was recommencing, and she was forced to seem to restore her attention to the orchestra and look straight forward.

When she could give another glance, he had moved away. He could not have come nearer to her if he would: she was so surrounded and shut in; but she would rather have caught his eye.

Mr Elliot's speech, too, distressed her. She had no longer any inclination to talk to him. She wished him not so near her.

The first act was over. Now she hoped for some beneficial change; and, after a period of nothing-saying amongst the party, some of them did decide on going in quest of tea. Anne was one of the few who did not choose to move. She remained in her seat, and so did Lady Russell; but she had the pleasure of getting rid of Mr Elliot; and she did not mean, whatever she might feel on Lady Russell's account, to shrink from conversation with Captain Wentworth, if he gave her the opportunity. She was persuaded by Lady Russell's countenance that she had seen him.

He did not come however. Anne sometimes fancied she discerned him at a distance, but he never came. The anxious interval wore away unproductively. The others returned, the room filled again, benches were reclaimed and repossessed, and another hour of pleasure or of penance was to be sat out, another hour of music was to give delight or the gapes, as real or affected taste for it prevailed. To Anne, it chiefly wore the prospect of an hour of agitation. She could not quit that room in peace without seeing Captain Wentworth once more, without the interchange of one friendly look.

In resettling themselves there were now many changes, the result of which was favourable for her. Colonel Wallis declined sitting down again, and Mr Elliot was invited by Elizabeth and Miss Carteret, in a manner not to be refused, to sit between them; and by some other removals, and a little scheming of her own, Anne was enabled to place herself much nearer the end of the bench than she had been before, much more within reach of a passer-by. She could not do so, without comparing herself with Miss Larolles, the inimitable Miss Larolles; but still she did it, and not with much happier effect; though by what seemed prosperity in the shape of an early abdication in her next neighbours, she found herself at the very end of the bench before the concert closed.

Such was her situation, with a vacant space at hand, when Captain Wentworth was again in sight. She saw him not far off. He saw her too; yet he looked grave, and seemed irresolute, and only by very slow degrees came at last near enough to speak to her. She felt that something must be the matter. The change was indubitable. The difference between his present air and what it had been in the Octagon Room was strikingly great. Why was it? She thought of her father, of Lady Russell. Could there have been any unpleasant glances? He began by speaking of the concert gravely, more like the Captain Wentworth of Uppercross; owned himself disappointed, had expected singing; and in short, must confess that he should not be sorry when it was over. Anne replied, and spoke in defence of the performance so well, and yet in allowance for his feelings so pleasantly, that his countenance improved, and he replied again with almost a smile. They talked for a few minutes more; the improvement held; he even looked down towards the bench, as if he saw a place on it well worth occupying; when at that moment a touch on her shoulder obliged Anne to turn round. It came from Mr Elliot. He begged her pardon, but she must be applied to, to explain Italian again. Miss Carteret was very anxious to have a general idea of what was next to be sung. Anne could not refuse; but never had she sacrificed to politeness with a more suffering spirit.

A few minutes, though as few as possible, were inevitably consumed; and when her own mistress again, when able to turn and look as she had done before, she found herself accosted by Captain Wentworth, in a reserved yet hurried sort of farewell. 'He must wish her good night; he was going; he should get home as fast as he could.'

'Is not this song worth staying for?' said Anne, suddenly struck by an idea which made her yet more anxious to be encouraging.

'No!' he replied impressively, 'there is nothing worth my staying for;' and he was gone directly.

Jealousy of Mr Elliot! It was the only intelligible motive. Captain Wentworth jealous of her affection! Could she have believed it a week ago; three hours ago! For a moment the gratification was exquisite. But, alas! there were very different thoughts to succeed. How was such jealousy to be quieted? How was the truth to reach him? How, in all the peculiar disadvantages of their respective situations, would he ever learn of her real sentiments? It was misery to think of Mr Elliot's attentions. Their evil was incalculable.

SEA AIRS AND SANDITON

From January to March 1817, Jane Austen was working on a new fiction set in a fashionable seaside town. But her health was rapidly failing, and she died in Winchester on 18 July.

The novel stops half-way through the twelfth chapter and was not published until 1925 as 'Fragment of a Novel' with a note that it was known to the Austen family as 'Sanditon'. Mr Parker is recovering from a carriage accident at the home of the Heywoods in rural Sussex. His hosts are persuaded to allow their daughter Charlotte to travel with Mr Parker and his family to Sanditon, the seaside town he is developing (sometimes identified as Worthing).

Commercial opportunities in coastal towns were not lost on the editors of *La Belle Assemblée*. Enterprising designer Mary Ann Bell took her 'trunk' to resort towns where 'the higher classes' bought her garments which were expressly invented for seaside pleasures. Here we have a dress that is easy to step in and out of when changing in a bathing machine. Bell's Circassian corset, launched in July 1814, offered 'relief and protection to pregnant ladies' advised to bathe, and her 'Chapeau Bras' sported on the head, although originally recommended for parties and the opera, is now given an airing at the seashore.

FASHIONS

FOR

AUGUST, 1814

EXPLANATION OF THE PRINTS OF FASHION

NO. I – THE CIRCASSIAN LADIES' CORSET BATHING AND SEA-SIDE WALKING DRESS

High dress of rich Indian or Parisian chintz, made in a form peculiarly novel and elegant; it is trimmed with chintz bordering to correspond, or a rich silk trimming. Long sleeve, with the fulness let in at the top. The collar is extremely novel and beautiful, and the trimming most tastefully disposed, so as to give the appearance of a shirt to the pelisse: it is loose in the body, but fastens in to the waist. We forbear a particular description of this elegant and convenient dress, as it must be seen to be properly understood; we have only to observe, that it is made in a form never before introduced, that it is equally tasteful and becoming; it enables a lady to dress herself in a few minutes without assistance, prevents the chance of taking cold by the long delay in dressing; and, when dressed, to look as completely fashionable as if she had employed the longest time at the toilet. The principal novelty, however, consists in Mrs. Bell's new invented Circassian corset, which unites the advantages of being conducive to health and comfort, by being made of novel materials, free from superfluities, such as steel, whalebone, or any hard substance: so that ease, gracefulness, and dignity are given to the female form in a manner perfectly novel and original. It gives relief and protection to pregnant ladies, and at the same time adds dignity and beauty to the appearance. Head-dress *Chapeau Bras*. Slippers of pale green; and gloves to correspond.

Circassian Ladies' Corset and Sea side Bathing Dress

Extract from
SANDITON

Upon the whole, Mr Parker was evidently an amiable family man, fond of wife, children, brothers and sisters, and generally kind-hearted; liberal, gentlemanlike, easy to please; of a sanguine turn of mind, with more imagination than judgement. And Mrs Parker was as evidently a gentle, amiable, sweet-tempered woman, the properest wife in the world for a man of strong understanding but not of a capacity to supply the cooler reflection which her own husband sometimes needed; and so entirely waiting to be guided on every occasion that whether he was risking his fortune or spraining his ankle, she remained equally useless.

Sanditon was a second wife and four children to him, hardly less dear, and certainly more engrossing. He could talk of it for ever. It had indeed the highest claims, not only those of birthplace, property and home: it was his mine, his lottery, his speculation and his hobby horse; his occupation, his hope and his futurity. He was extremely desirous of drawing his good friends at Willingden thither; and his endeavours in the cause were as grateful and disinterested as they were warm.

He wanted to secure the promise of a visit, to get as many of the family as his own house would contain to follow him to Sanditon as soon as possible; and, healthy as they all undeniably were, foresaw that every one of them would be benefited by the sea. He held it indeed as certain that no person could be really well, no person (however upheld for the present by fortuitous aids of exercise and spirits in a semblance of health) could be really in a state of secure and permanent health without spending at least six weeks by the sea every year. The sea air and sea bathing together were nearly infallible, one or the other of them being a match for every disorder of the stomach, the lungs or the blood. They were anti-spasmodic, anti-pulmonary, anti-septic, anti-billious and anti-rheumatic. Nobody could catch cold by the sea; nobody wanted appetite by the sea; nobody wanted spirits; nobody wanted strength. Sea air was healing, softening, relaxing – fortifying and bracing – seemingly just as was wanted – sometimes one, sometimes the other. If the sea breeze failed, the sea bath was the certain corrective; and where bathing disagreed, the sea air alone was evidently designed by nature for the cure.

His eloquence, however, could not prevail. Mr and Mrs Heywood never left home. Marrying early and having a very numerous family, their movements had long been limited to one small circle; and they were older in habits than in age. Excepting two journeys to London in the year to receive his dividends, Mr Heywood went no farther than his feet or his well-tried old horse could carry him; and Mrs Heywood's adventurings were only now and then to visit her neighbours in the old coach which had been new when they married and fresh-lined on their eldest son's coming of age ten years ago. They had a very pretty property – enough, had their family been of reasonable limits, to have allowed them a very gentlemanlike share of luxuries and change; enough for them to have indulged in a new carriage and better roads, an occasional month at Tonbridge Wells, and symptoms of the gout and a winter at Bath. But the maintenance, education and fitting out of fourteen children demanded a very quiet, settled, careful course of life, and obliged them to be stationary and healthy at Willingden.

What prudence had at first enjoined was now rendered pleasant by habit. They never left home and they had gratification in saying so. But very far from wishing their children to do the same, they were glad to promote *their* getting out into the world as much as possible. *They* stayed at home that their children *might* get out; and, while making that home extremely comfortable, welcomed every change from it which could give useful connections or respectable acquaintance to sons or daughters. When Mr and Mrs Parker, therefore, ceased from soliciting a family visit and bounded their views to carrying back one daughter with them, no difficulties were started. It was general pleasure and consent.

Their invitation was to Miss Charlotte Heywood, a very pleasing young woman of two-and-twenty, the eldest of the daughters at home and the one who, under her mother's directions, had been particularly useful and obliging to them; who had attended them most and knew them best. Charlotte was to go: with excellent health, to bathe and be better if she could; to receive every possible pleasure which Sanditon could be made to supply by the gratitude of those she went with; and to buy new parasols, new gloves and new brooches for her sisters and herself at the library, which Mr Parker was anxiously wishing to support.

All that Mr Heywood himself could be persuaded to promise was that he would send everyone to Sanditon who asked his advice, and that nothing should ever induce him (as far as the future could be answered for) to spend even five shilling at Brinshore.

FASHION GLOSSARY

Bodice – the upper part of a woman's gown or a quilted or boned undergarment
Bonnet – structured headwear for women for the outdoors with a brim and sides tied with strings or ribbons
Breast knot – material shaped into a bow or knot and pinned to the dress between the breasts

Cambric – a plain-weave soft linen or hand-spun cotton originally from Cambrai in France
Carriage dress – dress for travelling in a carriage, walking in gardens or promenading, usually high-necked, long-sleeved and loose-shaped for comfort
Cashmere (kerseymere, cassimere) – cloth made from the hair of the cashmere goat
'Chapeau Bras' – a face-framing hat designed by Mary Ann Bell
'Chip' straw – thin pieces of wood plaited or woven to construct sturdy bonnets
Circassian corset – a soft corset especially designed to lift and display breasts elegantly. 'Circassian' refers to the women from the Caucasus enslaved in Ottoman harems
Cloak – three quarter or full length outerwear
Clocks – fancy embroidery on stockings
Corset – an undergarment designed to form an elegant silhouette
Crape – light and transparent fabric, from wool or silk

CRAPE, CHINA – silk woven in India or China, now known as crêpe de Chine, used for evening dress and with tightly twisted fibres that achieve a crinkled effect

DEMI-TRAIN – a short train on a woman's garment with the back a little longer than the front

ERMINE – fur of a stoat native to Eurasia, associated with affluence and ceremonial dress
EVENING DRESS – clothing and accessories for evening events, SEE FULL DRESS

FICHU – a triangle or square of light fabric worn around the neck or chest
FLOSS – short fibres shed from silk cocoons in their winding and then used for decorative embroidery
FROCK – a gown with skirt and bodice attached to each other that fastens at the back
FULL DRESS – dress for formal occasions, primarily in the later afternoon or evening

GLOVES – white gloves; of white kid
GOWN – a dress, the main garment for a woman
GREEN, AMERICAN – a shade of light apple popular between 1800 and 1808
GYPSY HAT – straw hat with a flat crown and wide brim. Ribbons tied in a bow beneath the chin or at the back of the head held the hat in place from crown over the brim

HALF BOOTS – ankle-high boots usually for outdoor wear

HALF DRESS – less formal morning dress and afternoon walking dress

JACONET – a cotton of a weight between muslin and chintz
JANE – rose-coloured
JEAN – a tough, twilled cotton fabric
JONQUILLE – a yellow, the colour of daffodils

KERSEYMERE, *SEE* CASHMERE

LAPPETS – a pair of strips of material hanging from the top of the head down the back, often of lace
LENO – light but strong transparent cotton or linen
LIMERICK – fabric made from the tanned skins of unborn calves of an off-white or yellow colour which made a tight fit for gloves (sometimes referred to as 'chicken-skin' because they were so tight)

MANCHERON SLEEVES – short over-sleeves worn with day dresses or on top of an outer garment with long sleeves, resembling an epaulette
MANTLE – a cloak
MORNING DRESS – clothing worn at home at the time of day before visiting, often plain and white with a high collar and long sleeves
MUSLIN – cotton of a lightweight kind with an open weave which could be patterned, originating from India and later manufactured in Britain

NANKEEN – brownish-yellow coloured fabric originating from Nanjing, China

Pelisse – a coat-dress often fitted to the gown underneath
Polonese – an open robe that was not hitched up
Pomposas – square-toed boots
Promenade dress – another word for a walking dress, but more obviously worn for display. Worn during the London Season (spring and early summer) for shopping and strolling; in August and September at seaside resorts; and at country estates in the winter months

Redingote – a heavy coat that is double-breasted and with a high collar, a corruption of the French for 'riding coat' and could also refer to a long habit for riding
Ridicule aux getons – a small handbag or 'reticule' in which to store tokens
Robe – an evening gown that is open in the front to display the petticoat and with a train at the back
Round dress, Round gown – a gown with skirt attached to the bodice and the skirt closed all round, concealing the petticoat

Sarsnet (silk) – a soft silk that could be plain or twill and achieve different colours in its warp and weft
Scollop(ed) – an undulating edge to a fabric
Spencer, spenceret – a short jacket introduced in the 1790s to fit with the raised waistline of dresses named for the 2nd Earl Spencer. It was adapted from a man's double-breasted jacket. Most often an outdoor garment for the morning or afternoon
Sprig – pattern in the shape of a small flower or plant, embroidered or printed on a fabric
Stock – a long piece of cloth wrapped around the neck and fastened at the back

Tippet – a short cape like a stole or scarf

Toque – a brimless close-fitting hat sometimes as small as a headband, worn like a turban

Travelling dress – *see* Carriage dress

Tucker – lightweight material edging (muslin or lace) with a frill worn over a low neckline

Turban – length of fabric wrapped around a head or sewn in the style of Eastern headgear

Twist – plied silk thread for attaching buttons or decorating dress

Undress – casual or informal dress, mostly worn in the home

Vandyke – accessory with a v-shape inspired by collars worn in portraits by Anthony van Dyck

Walking dress – ensemble to wear outdoors and thus including headwear, an outer garment or wrap, and gloves

York tans – leather gloves in a buff colour that showed the dirt less than white or cream, used for walking or driving

Zephyr cloak – loose-fitting outer garment that will blow with the breeze (zephyr)

SOURCES & PERMISSIONS ACKNOWLEDGEMENTS

All images from *La Belle Assemblée*, excluding those on pp. 46 and 127, are reproduced from The National Library of Scotland, shelf mark FB.s.263.

The images on pp. 46 and 127 are reproduced from Special Collections and Archives, Templeman Library, University of Kent.

The illustrations on pp. 65, 69, 76, 137, 148, 158 and 167 are by Hugh Thomson.

Austen, Jane. *Letters of Jane Austen: With an Introduction and Critical Remarks* vols 1 & 2 (London: Bentley, 1884). A biography written by Jane Austen and her great-nephew, Edward Knatchbull-Hugessen, 1st Baron Brabourne.
———. *Jane Austen's Letters* (4th edn.), collected and edited by Deirdre Le Faye (Oxford: Oxford University Press, 2011)
———. *Teenage Writings*, edited by Freya Johnston and Kathryn Sutherland (Oxford: Oxford University Press, 2017)
Batchelor, Jennie and Manushag Powell. *Women's Periodicals and Print Culture in Britain, 1690–1820s. The Long Eighteenth Century* (Edinburgh: Edinburgh University Press, 2018)
Davidson, Hilary. *Dress in the Age of Jane Austen. Regency Fashion* (New Haven and London: Yale University Press, 2019).

———. *Jane Austen's Wardrobe* (New Haven and London: Yale University Press, 2023)

Hern, Candice. 'Regency World', Regency World Archive, CandiceHern.com [accessed December 2024]

Knight, Beatrice. 'All Things Regency', https://beatriceknight.com/mrs-bell/ [accessed December 2024]

ACKNOWLEDGEMENTS

This book is dedicated to the staff and trustees of Chawton House, the manor house in Hampshire once owned by Edward Knight, Jane Austen's brother, a stroll away from the cottage in the village that he provided for his sisters and mother and their friend, Martha Lloyd, from July 1809. This historic house, its rooms, gardens, exhibitions and collections – including a wonderful library of early modern books by women – is a place of inspiration: not only to me but many other scholars and visitors who walk in the footsteps of creative women, especially those of Jane Austen. I am honoured to be one of its trustees.

Thomas Robertson proved the most precise of research assistants and I am hugely grateful to him for his enthusiasm for the book and for Jane Austen.

Harriet Sanders has been throughout a responsive publisher, always believing in the project and making it better with her shrewd editorial eye. Daisy Dickeson's assistance has been invaluable in keeping things in order and securing images. Thanks also to Rachel Gambling, who first suggested investigating Regency fashion magazines alongside Jane Austen's fiction.

I have consulted the pages of *La Belle Assemblée* in numerous libraries and am grateful to the staff at the National Library of Scotland, Special Collections and Archives at the Templeman Library, Kent University (and especially Christine Davies), the British Library, the Bodleian Libraries and the Victoria and

Albert Prints and Drawings Study Room for their patience and sleuthing skills.

A loving, laughing family full of talent is, Jane Austen knew, the foundation of all happiness. I am lucky to have just such a family.

Ros Ballaster
Mansfield College,
University of Oxford